Dear Romance Reader,

Welcome to a world of breathtaking passion and never-ending romance.

Welcome to ***Precious Gem Romances.***

It is our pleasure to present *Precious Gem Romances,* a wonderful new line of romance books by some of America's best-loved authors. Let these thrilling historical and contemporary romances sweep you away to far-off times and places in stories that will dazzle your senses and melt your heart.

Sparkling with joy, laughter, and love, each *Precious Gem Romance* glows with all the passion and excitement you expect from the very best in romance. Offered at a great affordable price, these books are an irresistible value—and an essential addition to your romance collection. Tender love stories you will want to read again and again, *Precious Gem Romances* are books you will treasure forever.

Look for fabulous new *Precious Gem Romances* each month—available only at Wal★Mart.

Lynn Brown, Publisher

TAKE MY HAND

Adelaide Ferguson

Zebra Books
Kensington Publishing Corp.
http://www.zebrabooks.com

ZEBRA BOOKS are published by

Kensington Publishing Corp.
850 Third Avenue
New York, NY 10022

First Printing: March, 1999
10 9 8 7 6 5 4 3 2 1

Printed in the United States of America

To my tireless critique partner, Virginia Campbell Scott;
to my indispensable friend and adviser, Chris Rogers;
and to my husband Tom, who starved in the process.

ACKNOWLEDGMENTS

My thanks to my writing mentors: Rita Gallagher, Joan Reeves, Sharon Murphy, Barbara Kolaski, Audrey Compton, and Janet Miller, who never lost faith.

One

"Home free!" A pair of beige low-heel pumps sailed down the hall, and Allison McKay tossed her purse toward the table, surprised that it landed where she aimed. Glancing at the mirror in the foyer, she yanked the hairpins confining her sleek red chignon and shook her head like a frisky sorrel mare ready to play.

With one stockinged foot, she caressed the deep-pile, highly impractical white carpet, luxuriating in the sense of sanctuary she always felt when the door clicked shut behind her. Her gaze drifted over the lemon and white sofa she'd paid too much for, and the replica of a Tiffany lamp beside it. Her job with Graham Insurance Company allowed her to have most of the luxuries a confirmed couch potato could want, with enough left over to buy the retro clothes she adored.

Fluffing a puffy yellow cushion behind her, Allison propped her feet on the coffee table. A bottle of white wine left from several nights ago still stood on the small bar dividing the living room from the kitchen. Allison eyed the remaining four inches in the bottle doubtfully.

What the hell—live dangerously. Pouring a glass, she

leaned across the sofa and switched on the stereo, grimacing as the vinegary wine struck her tongue. After a sip or two, her nerves slowly unwound, and magically, the wine tasted better.

The soothing strains of a Chopin nocturne followed the path of clothing she shed on the way to the shower. Her stuffed white harp seal stared up at her from dolphin-print pillow cases with a fixed, button-eyed welcome.

"Hello to you, too," Allison said, stopping to drop a kiss on its black plastic nose.

Half an hour later, fresh from the shower, wet hair in a turban, and with a wildly colored paisley scarf belting her favorite 1940s green chenille bathrobe, Allison flopped down on the sofa.

Every weekend, she indulged her passion for collector clothes, wearing every goofy article she could find. From Friday night on, she was retro revisited. Somehow, wearing clothing from decades ago took the curse off her stiff, so-correct office wardrobe.

"The end of a perfect day!" Allison trilled, polishing off the last of the sour wine with scarcely a shudder.

One look at her feet propped on the coffee table convinced her that they were definitely feet—gorilla feet. *Gross!* If she meant to wear sandals tomorrow, she needed a pedicure.

The end table drawer produced a file, polish remover—but no cotton. Scouring the room, she noticed a scrap of plastic protruding from a Chinese temple jar by the door, and remembered what was in it. "Marshmallows!" Right where she'd left them six months ago on Halloween. When she lifted one out, it was rock hard.

"Perfect!"

She cast a wary glance toward the wall separating her from her new neighbors in 3B. If her luck held, they wouldn't start that thumping stereo again tonight. Ever since the new people had moved in two days ago, their deafening music had drowned out her beloved Chopin, shattering her peace and quiet.

Please, not tonight.

The week had been absolute hell, with her boss, Boswell Graham, sending constant memos to speed up her quarterly analysis of claims paid. Next week might be even worse. She cocked an ear toward the dividing wall. Still quiet. Maybe the 3Bs had gone out to howl at the moon instead of assaulting her ears.

Wedging a marshmallow between each toe, Allison selected Peach Blush polish and began applying a liberal coat to each toenail, skipping the clipping and filing this time. Who was to know? No one ever seemed to look past her flaming red hair anyway.

She examined her glistening toes with the stale marshmallows holding them apart.

"Twinkie toes," she chuckled.

Chopin's E-flat Nocturne filled the room, soothing Allison's tension like an expert masseuse. "Ahhh. Sweet peace." The wine and the music wrapped her in a dreamy, relaxing cocoon.

After fifteen minutes, she levered herself forward to test the polish. Still wet. She couldn't go to bed until the polish dried, or she'd have sheet marks on her toes in the morning.

Allison yawned hugely. Idly waving two fingers, she directed Claudio Arrau's skillful execution of the No. 4 Nocturne, wishing she had a little more wine.

Then a sudden blast of sound brought Allison upright, swamping the subtle music. A particularly loud blast sent vibrations through the walls and floor, jarring the coffee table beneath Allison's heels, making waves of pure rage surge through her. She turned up her own stereo louder, but it was about as effective as a kitten clawing at a tiger. Chopin remained hopelessly drowned beneath the incessant, ultra upbeat tune from next door. Whatever damned teenager lived there must have his amps turned up to Scream.

Allison's heart pounded wildly. Adrenalin caused a small vein to pulse in her temple.

"I'll fix that tone-deaf runt!"

Toes curled upward to spare the wet polish, Allison slammed through her front door and into the hall, stumping along on her heels. She paused and looked down at the ratty green chenille robe and remembered the turban she had on her head. Her scowl lightened into a fleeting grin. She looked pretty weird. Whoever was creating that demolition derby next door was in for a shock.

No one answered Allison's knock at 3B. She raised her fist to hammer on the door again, but before she could, a deep male voice called out, "Enter."

Startled, Allison lowered her fist. The crazed teenager's father must be at home. That sent her anger higher. Fists knotted, she would serve up general and particular hell to any adult who allowed his kid to make that much noise without regard for his neighbors.

The spirit of every McKay ancestor who ever went into battle before her converged in Allison's rigid body as she twisted the knob. To her surprise, the door was unlocked. What kind of fool left his door unlocked in the city? She paused uncertainly. Maybe her neighbors weren't afraid of intruders because *they* were the scary ones. Besides, what was she doing barging into a stranger's apartment with no idea what she might find?

She was about to turn around and go back when another blast of sound renewed her determination. Tightening the scarf at her waist, she thrust her chin in the air and charged through the door, blood roaring in her ears like super octane fuel in a high performance engine.

She skidded to a stop in the entry, squinting through the dimness.

Amber spots glowed softly from overhead. In misty topaz light, she made out the indistinct form of a tall man performing a strange, high energy dance in time to music blaring from the stereo—but his exotic movements weren't exactly a dance. They seemed to be some kind of controlled exercise.

Allison stared at the surreal scene. Maybe she'd dozed off after all. Maybe she was still lying on her sofa in 3A with four inches of wine under her belt. She passed her hand before her face.

When I look again, he'll be gone.

But he wasn't.

Moving farther into the room, Allison saw that the man was bare from the waist up. His finely contoured body wove through the amber glow like ivory through sheerest silk. He moved with fluid ease, his hands and feet keeping perfect time with the compelling beat of the music.

"The Power" blasted from the speakers, seeping into Allison's skin, pounding her body from head to toe. She felt as though she'd touched a high-voltage wire and couldn't let go. The beat became a physical pulse inside her. This man had the power all right, and Allison was absorbing every megadyne.

Heat radiated through her as the sensual performance continued. Strangely, the music no longer irritated her. She couldn't force her eyes from the hypnotically weaving figure in the center of the room. Even in the soft light, she could see dark brows etched above deep-set eyes in a classic face. A band around his head restrained sleek black, ear-length hair. As the man spun on one foot, she was treated to a wide sweep of shoulder and firmly muscled buttocks. His ankles never wavered as he executed the turn with perfect balance. Allison caught her breath. This man *was* power—and he was no teenager.

Abruptly, the music stopped and the man folded effortlessly to the floor in what Allison recognized as a lotus position she'd seen on TV yoga programs. Strange atonal flute music flowed from the speakers as the man remained seated, eyes closed, motionless. He gave no indication that he was aware of her hovering in the entry. He had withdrawn into himself, leaving Allison feeling as though a warming fire had been quenched. She was about to slip back through the door when the man's eyes opened.

"Don't go, please. I knew you were there, but I never interrupt my *kata* and meditation."

The linked series of karate moves and stances known as *kata* was not supposed to be seen by those outside the discipline, but the woman couldn't have known that when she'd barged in. And somehow he sensed that, from this moment, this bizarrely dressed woman he'd been hired to investigate and guard would become more than just an assignment.

Reaching for a towel, Jake slung it around his neck and drew off his headband, allowing his hair to fall free.

"Jake Tory," he said stiffly, adding a slight bow.

"Allison McKay," she replied, catching herself before she bowed back. She was suddenly acutely aware of her hideous appearance. "I shouldn't have barged in—"

"I know your name," Jake said, his voice uninflected and formally correct.

"You know? But how . . . ?" Allison slipped one foot behind her, imperceptibly edging toward the door. He must have read the name plate beside her mailbox. For the barest instant, she hoped he'd asked someone about her.

"I'm sorry if I disturbed you," Jake said gravely. "I sometimes lose myself in the exercise."

"Allison McKay. 3A, we're neighbors," Allison repeated needlessly. Self-consciously teetering on her heels, she passed a hand down her nubby green bathrobe. Weird was a good word for the way she looked—only now she wished she was wearing sleek leopard print leotards, belted with one of her Twenties scarfs, looking hot and sexy—not like a bag lady.

"I have to go. I'm—" She'd forgotten why she'd come in the first place.

"You are barefoot," Jake observed, making no reference to the marshmallows. "I approve—very healthy. I can't practice karate any other way."

Allison fidgeted, braiding her fingers nervously. He was so sexy—so calm and controlled—and she felt like something from the sale table at a swap meet. What could she say to this solemn man who looked her over as though weighing her on some scale of worthiness? Why didn't he loosen up, or get mad at her for barging in on him? Why didn't he laugh at her odd outfit? Anyone else would.

She wasn't angry any more. In fact, she felt like a tongue-tied ten-year-old. *Why can't I talk to this man like I would Herb or Boz, or any other man?* Because he wasn't *like* any other man. He was gorgeous.

The old saying about coming to scoff and remaining to pray was true. She'd come to give her new neighbor hell squared and had stayed, jazzed to the max, seduced by his extraordinary physical beauty and his magnificently coordinated movements.

Allison jammed her hands in her pockets. An unexpected jolt of desire nearly flattened her. Anyway, if this paragon among men passed her in the hall, he probably wouldn't recognize her in her office clothes.

"I'm really sorry I disturbed you," Jake said, contritely. "I'll practice at the dojang from now on." He followed closely as Allison backed toward the door.

"It's . . . don't bother, I . . . Good-bye," Allison squeaked, stumping for the door. But walking on her heels didn't help the lack of coordination that had made her a couch potato in the first place. She tripped on the threshold and fell flat on her face.

Scrambling up before Jake could reach her, Allison bolted into the hall at a run, scarlet with embarrassment. Behind her, she thought she heard Jake call out, but she kept running until she reached 3A.

Inside, Allison released the breath she hadn't realized she'd been holding. *Damn! Why did I have to fall on my face in front of that gorgeous man? Because I'm a klutz—always have been.*

Before she could scold herself further, there was a

knock on the door. Without thinking, she snatched it open, ready to blast anyone who came to the door this late.

Danger in the form of Jake Tory stood there, her apartment keys dangling from one finger.

From sheer reflex, Allison slammed the door in his face, wanting to hide. Appalled at what she'd done, she snatched the door open again. Though he gave no sign, she was sure the door had struck his bare foot.

"I think you dropped these." Jake paused. "Well, maybe they fell from your pocket." A slight smile teased one corner of his mouth. "I expect you'll be needing them." He extended the keys.

Allison slapped the pocket of her bathrobe. She'd left in such a fury, she'd failed to lock her own door behind her. Then she'd fallen down in Jake's doorway and lost her keys. Her face burned with humiliation. A man with Jake Tory's grace and bodily control must be laughing inwardly at a klutz like her.

"Thanks . . . I mean . . . well, thanks." She took the keys from Jake and tossed them toward the table beside the door, where they promptly slithered to the floor.

"Oh," Jake stopped her before she could close the door again, "I believe these are also yours." He extended four small marshmallows that must have dislodged from between her toes when she fell. Allison cursed herself silently, accepting the marshmallows.

"You could have just tossed them, but thanks anyway."

Jake nodded. "Good evening, Miss McKay." He turned back toward 3B. As he left, she detected the spicy scent of sandalwood.

Allison stared down at her feet. All but three marshmallows had vanished. She tested her polish. Dry enough for bed. She tilted her head to listen, but no sound came from next door.

What kind of man brought back stale marshmallows?

Two

"Request, my clavicle." Allison scowled at the memo on her desk. "A royal command is more like it." As much as she liked her boss, Boswell Graham, she knew that if she didn't show up for that self-defense demonstration, he'd have her on the intercom five minutes later.

After ten years with Graham Insurance, Boz ought to know physical exercise was somewhere in hell on Allison's agenda. She needed self-defense like a fish needed fresh air. She kicked the wastebasket. It rebounded and hit her shin, making her curse.

The memo requested all employees to attend the demonstration at two p.m. in the company recreation room. What was Boz thinking of? With the workload he'd handed her, he should know she couldn't spare the time. Besides, a devilish headache hammered her temples, she'd ripped the knee of her last pair of pantyhose on the desk drawer, and she had cramps. She was thoroughly annoyed at everything and everybody.

Her closest friend, Rhoda Felcher, bustled through the door waving her own copy of Boz's memo, and a brochure from a local martial arts school.

"Gonna check it out?" Rhoda eased her well-rounded hips into a chair beside the desk.

"Sorry, no can do." Allison's long, capable fingers massaged her throbbing temples. "You go witness the horrors of extreme physical exercise. You know perfectly well, I don't *do* sweating. I'd rather dive head-first through a meat grinder."

Rhoda pursed her lips. "No copping out this time, friend. Boz says muggings in the area are on the rise. He wants all of us to know how to defend ourselves—as if a good kick in the crotch wouldn't do the job. After all, you don't have to love self-defense to learn it."

Allison reached determinedly for a file.

"I haven't spent a lifetime lounging on the sofa for nothing. I don't want to ruin an unblemished record. I'll take my chances with the muggers."

"Yeah. Right," Rhoda snorted. "Come on, Allison. Loosen up. Just watching isn't contagious."

Ignoring Rho's remark, Allison read the open file. *Peter Martin. Extensive fire damage in kitchen area.*

The tenth fire claim this month, and all in the same area. Someone must be playing with matches. Allison wondered why Ross Curran, the claims adjuster, hadn't checked out these claims.

"It looks as though fires are right up there with muggings," Allison mused, shoving the top file toward Rhoda. "Maybe Boz should offer lessons in fire prevention.

Rhoda shoved the file back and rapped her knuckles on the desk. "Stop hiding behind work. I didn't come here to look at fire reports. You're coming to the demonstration with me," Rhoda said decisively. "Give this self-defense thing a chance! It might grow on you. Besides, the tae kwon do school is only a few blocks away." She pretended to adjust non-existent glasses, assuming a prissy tone, and reading aloud from the brochure in her hand. "Did you know that tae means foot, kwon means hand, and do means martial art? Tae kwon do is the Korean word for karate, and it's also known as the kick-punch method of defense. Now wouldn't you just love to kick-punch Ross Curran's butt?" Rhoda pronounced his name as if she were chewing on aluminum wrap.

Allison shrugged.

"Ross is a practicing pain in the neck, all right. He's also an ostentatious, supercilious louse, but I don't need lessons to handle him." She had dated Ross once, but never again. She didn't even remember how she had managed to get through the evening.

"You're still going to go to this tae kwon do. Hey, that rhymes," Rhoda said.

Allison sighed. Rho would nag until she agreed. Proof was in the black leather miniskirt and vest hanging in the back of Allison's closet, eye-opening price tags still attached, testifying to her best friend's persuasiveness.

"You'll be a knockout in black leather," Rhoda had insisted.

Yeah, right! And there was last year's swimsuit challenge. According to Rho's new diet, they'd both be wearing size eights by summer. Allison laughed to herself. Dear old Rho had finally confessed she'd sewn a size eight tag into her own size fourteen suit.

"Just think. We could get in shape on Boz's nickel, if we take that self-defense course," Rhoda wheedled. "Besides, what will I tell him if you don't show?"

Allison grinned. "I don't care."

"Oh, come on," Rhoda protested, her nose twitching indignantly. "You know I hate going anywhere alone."

"Face it. You're in denial. You go all over Houston alone. Besides, haven't you seen those guys on TV with no front teeth?" Allison folded her lips over her own teeth in a parody of a toothless man. "That's all we'd need to drive the guys wild—get our teeth kicked out in karate class."

Rhoda's brown eyes twinkled. "I'll take that for a yes." She darted toward the door before Allison could answer. "And, for your information," she called over her shoulder, "the no teeth look is ice hockey."

Allison leaned back, grinning. Round one to Rhoda. After all, she could just watch the demonstration. She needn't enroll. Even if she did enroll, she'd be thrown out after the first lesson the same way she'd been dropped from ballet class when she was eight.

Allison downed a couple of aspirin with cold coffee and reached for another file. She had a mountain of work to get through, if she was going to meet Rho for the two o'clock demonstration.

At a few minutes after two, Allison entered the company recreation room. Silhouetted against the light streaming through the window, the karate man stood arrow-straight and motionless. His absolute stillness drew Allison's eye. Calm, remote, he seemed buried within himself. Allison tried to make out his features. He was much taller than her own five foot eight, but she couldn't see his face against the glare.

Then he turned and a thrill coursed through her as his ebony gaze rested on her and she realized that the man on the platform was Jake Tory from 3B, her neighbor, the man who'd seen her in her . . . Embarrassment sent heat to her cheeks. She glanced quickly away. There was something unsettling about the self-contained, darkly handsome man. His powerful presence reached out to her. His very maleness screamed for attention, but his aura of aloofness signaled caution.

Allison drew back. *If she was lucky, he wouldn't recognize her.*

The demonstration had already started, and most of the seats were taken. She paused uncertainly in the doorway. She could still leave while the attractive Asian man at the mike explained the demonstration. His almond eyes, well spaced beneath dark slashes of brow, glowed with enthusiasm as he described the self-defense course offered for Graham employees.

Rhoda spotted Allison in the doorway and waved, pointing to a seat in the front row beside her. Abandoning the impulse to escape, Allison stepped forward, failing to notice the sound system wires near the door until a coil snaked around her ankle. Reaching blindly for support, she grasped the thick black cord leading to the amps. Suddenly, the sound went dead and Allison felt herself falling. Before she hit the floor, strong arms grasped her and set her on her feet.

"Are you all right, Miss McKay?" Jake asked quietly.

Allison nodded numbly, feeling his grip shift to her waist. Sparks of awareness prickled Allison's ribs where his arm made contact. He lifted her clear of the wire, his rock-hard forearm clasped just below her breasts. She stopped before she put her arms around his neck to steady herself. That jazzed feeling she'd had watching him exercise the night before was back, only more so now that their bodies met.

Allison glanced furtively at their audience. Everyone was staring at them. Boz craned his neck to see who had caused the interruption, and Rho was doubled over with laughter. Ross Curran stared scornfully, a scowl marring his shirt-ad features. But the Asian man holding the dead mike seemed unperturbed as he waited patiently for sound to be restored.

"Thanks," Allison managed to whisper. "I'm sorry." She twisted in her rescuer's arms. Up close, Jake was even more drop-dead handsome than she'd first thought. Long lashes shaded his midnight eyes. She felt his warm breath against her cheek and fought an insane urge to reach up and draw his mouth to hers.

When he smiled, white teeth contrasted with his tanned features. Something in Allison's stomach flipped and dropped to that place where lovers meet. He was the most magnetically sexy man she'd ever encountered—and this was, she reminded herself, just an accidental encounter.

Rho's rule was, "Watch out for the lookers—they're toxic." If that was true, then Jake Tory was a megadose of exactly the kind of poison Allison didn't need right then.

For a moment longer, Jake held her.

"Is that your seat?" he asked, nodding toward the vacant place next to Rhoda.

"I guess it is now. Thanks. I'll just—" Allison tried to laugh, but Jake's body heat radiating against the length of her stole her breath. He'd called her Miss

McKay. He recognized her as the same weird woman who stomped into his apartment with marshmallows between her toes.

The karate man didn't seem the least affected by the roomful of eyes on them—or by her.

Marshmallow toes. Jake hid a smile. *Girl of my dreams.*

When he released her and returned to the stage, Allison felt that same chill she'd felt when he left her before—as though a fire had been extinguished.

Too late to worry about making a disturbance, Allison picked her way to the front row, her heart still pounding, her mind's eye imprinted with Jake's all-male image.

Heat radiated in her cheeks. She hadn't blushed this much since she was in the sixth grade when Cleat Jensen brought her a wilted daisy and told her she was the prettiest girl in class, but she was blushing now, and over a complete stranger. When she glanced up again, the karate man had joined his partner at the microphone.

"That's a novel way to meet a guy," Rhoda whispered after Allison sank down beside her.

Her answer was a sharp elbow in Rho's ribs. Rho insisted her own guy was out there somewhere and she would find him. Until she did, she would keep on shopping. Following the direction of Rhoda's gaze, Allison decided that, if Rho was shopping today, the handsome Asian man at the mike must be sale day at Macy's.

Allison folded her hands in her lap to listen to the speaker, who said his name was Kim Joon.

With sound restored, Kim Joon introduced Allison's neighbor as his partner in the local martial arts school. Jake bowed solemnly to the audience, sending Allison a glance seemingly meant only for her. Then turning, he bowed to Kim Joon.

The two men began to move with leopard-like grace, slowly, without force, demonstrating each defensive move and explaining its use. Allison's pulse raced as she watched Jake Tory's superbly honed body move . . . if only his eyes didn't darken from a deep rich brown to black before she could decide which they were. His graceful movements affected her like a gently stroking hand on her body. Her breathing became shallow and ragged. Her powerful, immediate response to the man stunned Allison. She reminded herself that someone like Jake Tory could never be interested in a career woman with no athletic skills whatsoever. Besides, he probably already had some beautiful, hard-bodied babe at home.

Allison glanced at Ross, who still stared straight ahead, a condescending smirk on his lips.

She concentrated on the brochure in her lap. From the address shown, the karate school must have taken over the old Pier One site in Corinth Center, three blocks from Graham Tower—and only two blocks from her apartment. At least, the location was convenient, should she ever decide . . . Forget it, she told herself. She had to make that swap meet early and nail down the lace collar she'd been coveting.

The two men worked as though their minds were one, but Allison only saw Jake Tory. She couldn't understand, nor explain the immediate connection she felt with him. Did he feel it, too?

When the group broke up, Rhoda tapped Allison's shoulder.

"Hey! Are you in there?" She nodded toward Jake. "Not too hard to take, is he?"

Allison tore her gaze from the platform. Women were already gathering, asking questions just to get Jake to notice them.

"Don't be silly, Rho, I was just—" She had no intention of getting interested in a martial arts instructor, regardless of the effect this particular one had on her.

"My spleen! I know you were *just.* Listen, I don't blame you, but guard your heart against the handsome ones."

"Him? I wasn't . . . besides, my heart doesn't need guarding." Allison's face was flushed—and Rho noticed.

"You're lying!" Rho chortled. "Just be sure you shop around. But make a note, friend. The Asian guy's mine!" Rhoda's full-bodied laughter rang through the auditorium. In a lower tone, she said, "Remember, Allison, honey, Jake Tory's a beautiful man, but he could be a heartbreaker."

Or he could be the love of my life, Allison thought, then banished the idea. What on earth had made her think such a ridiculous thing? All her energy was dedicated to career advancement, nothing else. She didn't want a man in her life right now. What she wanted was that promotion—the one Ross Curran was so damned sure *he'd* get.

Her lips twisted in a wry grin. "I'm too old to need a mother, Rho," she said. She hadn't needed one since Mom died when she was ten, and Dad dumped her on Aunt Helen and took off. "I'm well able to—"

"Like I should believe you?" Rhoda's hand came down on Allison's arm. "Just be careful, Allie. Life is full of potholes, and if anyone's gonna step into one, it'll be you."

Jake Tory had turned at the sound of Rhoda's laughter. For a moment, his gaze locked with Allison's before she turned away to reach for her purse.

"For Pete's sake, let's go." She snatched up the purse and stepped toward the door. "I have tons of work before the weekend."

Rhoda continued her study of Kim Joon. "Obsessive. That's what you are, Allison McKay. Obsessive." Her eyes remained glued to the handsome Korean man. "Leave all that crap for Monday."

"You stay. I'm outta here." Allison slung her purse strap over her shoulder and headed for the door. She had to escape.

"Remember," Rhoda called after her, "First self-defense class starts at noon Saturday at the Tory-Joon Dojang."

"Maybe," Allison muttered, aware that Jake's eyes followed her. He seemed to be waiting for her reply. The thought of seeing Jake Tory again on Saturday both frightened and exhilarated her. *I'm overreacting.* It was only a self-defense course. No biggie. She risked a sideways peek at the platform. Jake was no longer looking her way.

"Noon tomorrow," she called back, deciding on the instant. With a final glance at her friend's rapt features, Allison wondered if Rho's shopping expeditions might finally be over.

"Did you see that foxy blonde in the front row?" Kim Joon asked Jake.

"No." Jake continued packing their gear without looking up. "But I *did* see a vision with red hair and cat-green eyes." He could still feel Allison's soft curves in his arms, her warmth against his body. She fit him as though she'd been made to be there. He'd never reacted so powerfully to a woman. Dressed up, or ragged as a beggar, she was staggeringly sexy. He hadn't wanted a woman—*really* wanted a woman—in his life. Oh, he'd had casual affairs, but no woman had reached out to him the way Allison McKay did.

Jake thought of his *sensei's* teaching: the master of martial arts is master of himself. That had always been Jake's rule of life, but the moment he'd caught the woman he'd been assigned to guard in his arms, something inside said she was the one he'd been waiting for.

Jake recalled his meeting with Boswell Graham the week before.

"Sit down, Tory." Graham had motioned Jake to a chair. "Thanks for coming."

"My pleasure, sir." Jake waited quietly for Graham to proceed.

"I'm going to level with you. The self-defense classes are a cover-up so you can investigate a theft in the company."

Jake leaned forward. "Give me someplace to start." He'd fished for a pen and opened his notebook.

"Only two of my people could have pulled this off."

"Exactly what would you want me to do?"

For a moment, Graham's steady blue eyes rested on Jake, then he seemed to reach a decision.

"Someone in the company is falsifying fire claims and certifying payments to John Doe accounts. The John Doe names keep changing before the data entries catch up. Four million dollars have already disappeared. But our thief wasn't quite fast enough this time, and all entries are current." Graham peered over his glasses at Jake.

"Four million and two suspects?" Jake whistled softly. "Have you notified the police?"

"No police. The thief might run."

Jake nodded.

Graham relaxed back into his chair. "Then you'll take on the investigation?"

"It's what I do."

Graham slid a contract across the desk. "We need to move quickly, Tory. Is this satisfactory?"

Jake glanced down at the paper and nodded. The sum offered was magnificent.

"Only you and your partner will be in on the company's problem."

"I understand, sir." Jake tucked the contract in his pocket.

"I want surveillance on Ross Curran, senior claims adjuster, and Allison McKay, our claims auditor."

"Descriptions, please." Jake kept his tone neutral.

Graham flipped a photograph of Curran across to Jake.

The guy could be a department store dummy. Jake grinned to himself. This one wouldn't want his clothes wrinkled.

The picture of Allison McKay made Jake's heart stop. Her heavy red hair was caught in a smooth chignon, her green eyes looked directly at the photographer, and what was visible of her upper body was any man's dream. Jake studied the photo a moment longer. Allison McKay couldn't be a thief.

Graham tossed a set of keys to Jake.

"We've rented an apartment for you next to Miss McKay. I want you to let me know where she goes, who she sees after work. I want a detailed record of her movements—but most important, look after her."

"You don't want Miss McKay to be guilty, do you?"

"Frankly, no," Graham said. "Furthermore, I don't believe she is. Help me prove it, Tory."

Jake nodded his assent.

"Allison may prove to be a problem," Graham warned. "She'll try to weasel out, if she can. It will be up to you to persuade her to take your classes."

"I'll handle it," Jake said shortly. If the woman didn't show up, he'd go get her.

Three

Allison wavered uncertainly between the kitchen and the bedroom. She could skip food and go to bed, or— Before she could decide, the phone rang.

"Allie!" Rhoda squealed. "What happened to our ice cream orgy? You said you'd call."

Allison's encounter with Jake Tory had erased everything else from her mind, but this was Rho's designated night to shoot the works on calories.

"Sorry, hon, I forgot. I had a headache." At least that part was true. "How about tomorrow? I'm passing up my swap meet for that damn karate class you muscled me into. We could pick up some ice cream after class—unless I'm too crippled to lift a spoon."

Rhoda tapped her fingernail against the phone. "You don't sound so good, Allie. Haven't I told you ice cream is guaranteed to cure anything from heartache to hives? What do you say?"

Allison forced a laugh. "I'm fine, really. I just need to collapse into bed."

"Sure I can't tempt you?"

"Thanks, but I'll pass. Let's wait for a real crisis to sacrifice our hips." As much as she loved Rho, she wished she'd hang up.

Rho mumbled around what sounded like another

mouthful of ice cream. "Don't forget. Noon tomorrow. Self-defense class."

"How can I forget? You won't let me—" The line went dead. Rho's ice cream must be melting.

Allison dropped the phone in its cradle and sank down on the sofa. So much had happened in a matter of hours, her mind was still reeling. She never would have believed she'd be taking self-defense lessons, or find herself living next door to the sexy Jake Tory who would teach her. Nor could she have imagined the interview she'd had with Boz after the demonstration. She had no sooner returned to her office than the intercom had buzzed.

"Allison? Can you come up, please?"

Why was Boz calling her so late on Friday? He should be on the golf course by now.

Once on the twelfth floor, Allison left the elevator and entered Boz's executive office.

He met her at the door.

"Thanks for coming, Allison." Boz pointed to a chair. His angular features were pleated with concern, and his Texas-blue eyes were clouded beneath unruly, sun-blasted brows. His shock of blond-gray hair seemed to have been plowed more than once that day, and not harrowed back into place. He seemed edgy. The atmosphere was as heavy as an impending tornado.

"Who died?" she asked, easing into the chair.

Boz sat down and leaned toward her.

"What I have to say may shock you, but here it is: I have reason to believe Ross Curran is a thief."

Allison's eyes widened. "I knew Ross was a certified crash dummy, gold medal dork, and jerk of the century—but a thief?"

"Let me explain." Boz shoved a file across the desk. "Is this your signature?"

Allison nodded. "I signed this, but what has that to do with Ross being a thief?"

"We believe Curran intends to use this file, and others like it, to blackmail you into helping him get away with the money he's stolen from the company."

For a moment, she couldn't speak. The very audacity of the idea staggered her.

"Blackmail me! But, Boz, I sign claims like these every day. There must be zillions out there. How can he—"

"First, let me say that I know you're innocent of any wrongdoing—but Curran doesn't *know* I know. He thinks he can steal from the company and make you take the fall. He'll make it appear you signed false claims to John Doe accounts in order to collect the money for yourself. The only difference is, it's Ross who's been doing the collecting. We've been watching him for some time, but we need hard evidence."

Allison stared. How could this be happening? Ross wasn't smart enough to pull off something like this.

"The files Ross brought me looked just like dozens of others I've approved." Then she remembered the ten fire claims occurring in a very short time—all the way from River Oaks to the ship channel.

"These particular claims were anything but ordinary, Allison. In fact, I suspect arson." At her gasp, Boz reached for her hand and squeezed it reassuringly. "These were real policyholders—until Curran forged fictitious names in place of the real claimants. At first, we thought it was Herb Miller. It's his job to place the final seal on a claim before it can be paid, but he was ruled out almost immediately. The company seal is too closely guarded. But if Herb saw your signature, he wouldn't hesitate to sign off on the claim. Between you and Ross, there was never a question." Boz stood and began pacing, rubbing his head as though all the answers were hidden there, if he could just jar them loose.

Allison sat deathly still as reality seeped into her consciousness. "Then I'm really the one responsible. I should have been more alert—"

"Don't fret," Boz said, shaking his head. "Nothing will happen to you, but I need your help."

"Ross knows I despise him. He'd be suspicious of me from the get go."

Boz raised a hand. "Let me finish. It's the John Doe payees we're focusing on. We need to know if Curran kept the same payee names to set up bank accounts for each—and where."

"He'll never tell me!" Allison's voice rose as nerves took over.

"Allison, you're the only one who *can* do this." Boz removed his glasses and fixed her with a level gaze. "As long as Curran thinks he can blackmail you, he'll expect you to do anything to protect yourself. He knows you're the only one at Graham who can testify against him. You can tell how he solicited your signoffs on these John Doe claims."

Boz passed a hand wearily across his eyes. He seemed to have aged within the hour. Allison knew darn well she had.

"Try to convince him you're greedy. Make money the reason for your change of heart toward him. Convince him it would be in his interest to take you with him, share the money, before you're arrested.

He won't want the spotlight on himself just when he's about to split." Boz squeezed Allison's shoulder gently. "And I want you to go through with the self-defense course."

Allison sat in stunned silence. From a routine life, she'd been catapulted into some sort of undercover scheme to catch an embezzler. "What good will self-defense classes do?" Allison protested. Boz started to answer, but Allison put up a hand. "I know. You're going to tell me I need the exercise."

"Not this time," Boz said, his expression sober.

"Why am I not surprised to learn Ross is a thief?" Allison mused. "But a blackmailer?" She despised Ross Curran and he knew it. But her mind already chased ideas to dupe him into believing she was as dishonest and greedy as he was.

Boz turned away. "Trust me, Allison. Nothing bad will happen to you in all this."

Allison's stomach plunged. Why did Boz keep mentioning her safety? What wasn't he telling her?

A rose-scented candle worked its magic on Allison's frazzled nerves, drawing her back to her own safe world. Her sometime-psychic friend, Peggy from the accounting department, said pink candles drew angels. Allison could use a few angels right now. She was genuinely scared.

She was about to head for the kitchen to raid the fridge when she heard someone at the door.

"I hope it's not too late." Jake Tory leaned against the door frame, two bottles of spring water dangling between his fingers.

Allison made a quick sweep of the room, looking

for litter, dirty plates, empty wine bottles. Her shoes were propped at a cockeyed angle against the sofa, and the TV program guide was jammed between the sofa cushions.

"No . . . not too late. Come in." She stumbled backwards, banging against the table beside the door. The Chinese temple jar teetered dangerously, but Jake deftly caught it and returned it to its place.

"I thought we might get better acquainted—since we're neighbors and you'll be taking my class." Jake lifted one dark brow. "You will be coming to class in the morning, won't you?"

Allison groaned. "I promised Rhoda, but I can't be sure how long I'll stay. You'll probably ask me to leave anyway when you see me in action." She wouldn't shy away from Jake's classes, just because he'd stirred long-buried needs.

"Good." As though he belonged there, Jake walked over to the sofa and sank down, waggling the spring water bottles between his fingers. "Glasses? Or do you prefer drinking from the bottle—while standing in the doorway?"

"Oh . . . no—" Allison started forward, then stopped to be sure nothing was in her path to trip over.

The candle's flame reflecting in the mirror cast subtle light across Jake's tanned features, drawing her toward him until she stopped herself.

"Hang on. I'll get glasses." Allison stopped just inside the kitchen. Were there any clean glasses? A search of the cabinet yielded two lone jelly jars with Disney characters printed on the sides. What the hell. So she saved "collector" glasses. So she ate junk food and wore retro clothes. Properly defensive, she marched back into the living room and handed Jake the jars.

After a careful inspection of the Lion King characters on each glass, Jake looked up and smiled. "Kim and I saw the movie in Honolulu. Great animation." He halved one bottle between them and handed Allison hers, stretching his long legs out beneath the coffee table. "We used to manage a martial arts school there."

"Really." Allison felt like a fool, standing in her stocking feet in the middle of the living room, making small talk and sipping from a Lion King glass in the company of a man whose sex appeal was dynamite.

The only place to sit was beside Jake, and his athletic frame claimed most of the space. A shaky feeling rattled around in Allison's stomach like dice in a backgammon cup. Something told her that, if she got too near this karate man's fire, she'd be burned badly—and the scars could be permanent.

"Um, Jake—you said you wanted to talk about class tomorrow. What did you want to tell me?"

"Tell you? Nothing really. I came to make sure you'd show up. Your boss wants you there—and I want you there."

How did he know Boz wanted her there?

"Why me in particular?" Were they in some kind of conspiracy?

"Mr. Graham likes you. He thinks you need more exercise," Jake said, studying her body somewhat critically.

"I'll decide when I need more exercise." She was furious with Boz. Everything he'd said was supposed to be confidential, but evidently he'd spoken to Jake Tory about her.

Allison reached for the second bottle of spring water and wrenched the cap off, splashing half its contents in Jake's lap.

"Here. Let me do that." He took the bottle and topped off their glasses and set the bottle aside. "Why are you so nervous, Allison?" he asked softly. His tone was that of a . . . relative . . . close friend . . . a lover? She struggled to breathe.

"I'm not—"

"You're as edgy as a cat." He placed a warm palm at her nape and began a gentle massage. "I won't hurt you. In fact, I'll teach you how not to get hurt."

Allison felt trapped but pleasurably so. The hypnotic feel of his broad palm against her neck made her want to stay this way forever. He probably meant *physically* hurt. That wasn't what she feared.

"How often do you think I'll need to know that?" She gulped her water and nearly choked. "Hasn't anyone told you I'm a certified couch potato? Unless there are drooling perverts at the swap meets I attend every Saturday, it's not very likely I'll need to defend myself. But then," she pretended to consider, "when two women both want to buy the same thing—"

"I see you're not going to talk sense about this." Jake lowered his mouth to hers, closing off any further debate.

Allison pressed closer, slipping her arms around Jake's broad shoulders, deepening the kiss, fitting her body to his. She shouldn't be doing this, but just this once . . .

Her body responded with a primal urgency. She wanted Jake to make love to her. She *needed* Jake to make love to her.

Then she felt him draw away.

"I shouldn't have done that," he said. "I just . . . look, Allison, we're adults. We'd be liars not to admit there's something between us." His fingertip traced her kiss-swollen lips.

Allison's arms slid from Jake's shoulders, fighting for breath, wanting more, but knowing she wasn't going to get it.

Jake set her gently aside and stood. "As they say in the TV movies, to be continued."

She followed him to the door, still dazed by what had just happened.

At the door, he lifted her chin. "Good night, neighbor." He dipped his head and kissed her gently. Before she could react, he was through the door, drawing it closed behind him.

The feel of Jake's kisses lingered long after he was gone. He was right. There was something between them. She'd known it from the first. Why must the man be so damned sexy—and live so temptingly near?

A hot cup of decaf might help bring back some of her usual level-headedness. She headed into the kitchen to make some, and took her sweet time about it.

Slipping into her scruffy green bathrobe, Allison sat down to have her coffee. She picked at a chenille thread dangling from the raised pattern, unraveling one of the nubs and leaving a bald spot. *Damn!* She couldn't let her attraction to Jake Tory sidetrack her from getting out of Ross's blackmail trap. But on the other hand . . .

Allison forced herself to concentrate on the gorgeous lace collar she'd wanted to buy this weekend.

The collar would probably be gone by Sunday . . . but Jake would still be here.

His dark gaze haunted her. And she couldn't shake the memory of his hard, athlete's body crushing her against him. When she saw him tomorrow, she would stay in the back of the exercise room and pay special attention to where she stepped. She would watch Kim Joon and keep clear of Jake.

"Yeah? And who's supposed to believe that?" she muttered, running a hand down the curve of her hip. Soft. Not a muscle anywhere. Jake Tory's woman would have a hard body. She'd probably jog and eat bean sprouts instead of burritos, and she'd know all about tae kwon do. She'd be blond and gorgeous and never trip over electrical cords.

Allison grimaced in disgust. She was none of those things.

She made a vampire cross with her fingers toward the wall dividing 3A and 3B. She would stop thinking about Jake Tory. She definitely would. He was only a man. An indecently handsome man, but only a man. So what if he was every girl's dream? If she wasn't careful, he could become this girl's worst nightmare.

Levering herself off the sofa, Allison took her empty cup to the kitchen. Her dinner options were slim to none. Last week's pizza slices hadn't developed mold yet, so she nuked one and choked it down with a half glass of soda. The pizza stopped somewhere just below her windpipe and refused to go lower.

After several lady-like burps, she loaded the week's assortment of dirty plates into the dishwasher and returned to the empty living room. With Jake no longer there, her perfect sanctuary suddenly felt as empty as an abandoned warehouse.

In 3B, Jake stripped off his T-shirt and stretched out on the futon sleeping mat he'd placed at the foot of a treasured black lacquered screen, a Korean antique. A hairline crack in the ceiling caught his gaze. Like his own solitary life, the crack wouldn't have been visible to the casual observer—until now.

A sudden chill made Jake draw the lightweight cover higher. He rolled onto his stomach, and allowed his gaze to trace the intricate Oriental characters etched on the screen above him. "Long life, a good wife, and many children." Would that ever be true for him?

The soft glow of track lights conjured images of Allison lying on the futon beside him. He shouldn't have kissed her, but he couldn't help it. She was so inviting—so all woman—and everything he'd ever wanted.

He smiled at the ceiling. Allison reminded Jake of a wobbly colt that needed steadying—his steadying. He recalled her stumbling through his apartment door. He thought of her hollow bravado and her stubborn, admirable determination to do things for herself.

With a soft groan, he rolled onto his back and folded his arms beneath his head, willing himself to relax, but sleep eluded him.

A lifetime of training from a remote, polite *sensei* had prepared him for life's deadlier happenstances, but had left him totally unprepared to tell a woman he wanted her.

Jake's thoughts lingered on Allison's long, silky red hair and her gemlike green eyes. He imagined her willowy body beneath his hands, his fingers stroking her heavy mane while he kissed her. With a sigh, he sat up. He hardly knew the woman and he was fantasizing about her night and day.

He sought peace in meditation as always, but before he lost himself completely, a tingle of anticipation intruded.

Tomorrow he would see Allison again.

Four

Allison gazed up at the indecipherable brushstroke characters slashed in black across the white facade of the Corinth Center building. Beneath the strange letters was a sign she could read: "Tory-Joon Dojang." She felt a strange reluctance to go inside, and wished now she hadn't let Rho persuade her into coming.

Taking a deep breath, she pressed open the door. She was met by a young boy in loose cotton pants and jacket. He pointed to her feet, motioning for her to remove her shoes.

Allison gave the boy an uncertain smile. She wished she'd followed her first instinct and headed for the swap meet. As she turned to leave, Jake Tory emerged from his office, clad in a white jacket and trousers identical to the boy's, only his narrow waist was cinched with a black belt with red fringe on the ends. His finely shaped, high-arched feet were bare—and he looked sensational.

"Welcome," Jake said, easing between Allison and the door. "Jimmy will take care of your shoes." Numbly, Allison handed the boy her shoes, feeling as if some alien force had taken her over.

"Come with me." Jake stepped aside for Allison to enter. "You were late for the demonstration at work.

Everyone else filled out enrollment papers then. Now I need yours." He went behind the desk and pulled out a blank form.

Allison glanced warily around for objects she might trip over, then chose a chair and sat down. Jake seemed so formal. Nothing like the man who had come bearing spring water and kisses the night before. Today, he made her feel like a school kid reporting to the principal without her homework. And why was he so sure she *wanted* to sign up for his class? If she hadn't felt obligated to Boz . . .

She desperately wanted a place to hide her bare feet, and wound up scooting them under the edge of the desk.

"If you will complete this, please." Jake slid a printed form toward her.

"Yes. Of course." She heard her traitorous self agreeing. Jake leaned back in his chair, his head to one side, waiting patiently while she clicked out the pen and bent over the form. She stole a glimpse from the corner of her eye. She'd been right. He was all gold and ivory. Her eyes fixed on his lips. He caught her looking and looked right back. The thought of six weeks in the company of the man across from her made her heart do flip-flops.

Weight? Guess. Age? Guess again. Why did he need answers to such personal questions? She wasn't here to become the next Miss Universe. Shoving the form across the desk, she forced herself to meet his eye squarely.

He glanced at the form, filling in the spaces she'd left blank. Graham had already given him the answers, plus a lot more.

"One hundred twenty-five pounds, 5′10″, general health good, age twenty-six."

"How did you know all that? I didn't write it down."

"Psychic." Before they were through, he'd know a lot more about her than her dimensions. "Did you bring workout clothes?" he asked coolly, eyeing the black and jade jogging outfit she had on.

"What's wrong with these?" Allison unzipped her jacket to reveal a sleeveless jade cotton tank top. "I hadn't really meant to stay. I just dropped by because I promised Rho I would."

"I'm glad you changed your mind. You won't be sorry." The look Jake sent her would melt a rock. "You can wear this *gi*. This is the uniform I issue to tae kwon do students when they enter the discipline. And this is your *ti*." He extracted the woven white belt from the package and handed it to her. "Suit up. We're about to start." He pointed toward a sign marked WOMEN, and without a backward glance, headed for the practice room.

Allison eyed the baggy garments Jake had given her. Why couldn't she wear what she had on? Once she got this *gi* thing home, she decided she'd jazz it up a little, add some color—get rid of the white sash. One of her antique scarves might work. The green and gold paisley. Yes.

In less than ten minutes, Allison was dressed and feeling like the biggest fool this side of Barnum & Bailey. The *gi* fit her perfectly, but damned if she knew how to tie the sash to look like Jake's. It hung down the front of her jacket like wet wash. She flipped the ends of the woven belt disgustedly. A scarf would definitely be better, and she knew how to tie scarves.

Beside the door to the main room, Allison noticed a red honeycombed box with numerous pairs of shoes resting in the tiered slots, her own among them. She wiggled her toes and made a sour face. What harm could wearing sneakers do? This martial arts stuff was terminally weird.

When she entered the mirrored practice room, Rhoda hurried to meet her. Her uniform was identical to Allison's, only her belt was neatly tied.

"You came!" Rhoda squealed. "You should have let me know; I would have picked you up."

"Thanks, but I value my life too much to ride in your car," Allison chuckled. Rhoda drove her dented red Taurus like a maniac and, to Allison's absolute amazement, never got a ticket. If Allison fudged a single stop sign, she'd get nailed.

Rhoda made a few style moves, turning like a runway model.

"What do you think? Is it me?"

"Cool," Allison drawled, "but somehow I don't think we'll make any Best Dressed lists." Her bare ankles looked pretty silly in the mirror. She looked like a stork in the loose-fitting pajamas Jake had called a *gi*. Next time, she'd wear something hotter and brighter—something that made her feel more like herself. She mentally rummaged through her antique clothes closet. She'd find something really cute and bring an outfit for Rhoda as well. Then, all at once, she realized she'd committed herself to the class.

"Tae kwon do is a beautiful discipline," Kim Joon was saying as Allison and Rhoda approached a small group. "Jake and I have devoted our lives to the art, and we hope that many of you will want to continue your studies once this course is over."

Although Kim addressed the class, his eyes never left Rhoda. When he finished speaking, he went to stand beside Jake.

Jabbing Rhoda to drag her eyes away from Kim, Allison whispered, "Coming here was a big mistake. Why can't I just be the couch potato I was born to be?"

"Get over it!" Rhoda muttered.

Allison shrugged. What was six weeks in the life of a fool? Six weeks max and she was out of here. She had no intention of devoting her time to some bone-jarring routine she didn't need in the first place.

Kim smiled, extending a palm for Allison and Rhoda to join him, but Jake stepped into his path.

"I'll take Miss McKay in my group," he said quietly. For a moment, Kim eyed Jake curiously, then led Rhoda away.

Jake's manner was brisk as he explained the stylized movements, some of which, he cautioned, could become lethal blows.

Allison couldn't believe Jake had chosen her for his group—especially after she'd fallen flat in his apartment, slammed the door on his foot, and spilled spring water all over him. She had planned to hide out in the back of the room until class ended.

Jake's unreadable eyes swept the group, their power dragging everyone, including Allison, into his magnetic aura. An odd feeling of sensual lethargy claimed her. She was content just to watch Jake's lips move, feeling, rather than hearing, his liquid voice wash over her—remembering his kiss.

She sat down and grasped her ankles in an effort to stretch her legs on either side of her body the way Kim and Jake managed so easily. She felt like a wishbone on Thanksgiving.

"Tory lives in 3B," Allison whispered to Rhoda, who had settled into Kim's foursome next to her. "I'll tell you later." She strained to bend her forehead to her knee. Her groin muscles screamed in protest. Things had to get better.

Rhoda spread her short, plump legs wide and groaned aloud, drawing Kim's concerned glance. Allison felt a wave of satisfaction. Rho couldn't do it either. Her round little tummy got in the way.

"Who tied your sash for you?" Allison struggled upward to wave the ends of her own sash at Rhoda.

"Kim," Rhoda puffed. "He's my guy, Allie. I knew it the minute I saw him. Now, all I have to do is convince him that he can't live without me."

Allison studied Rho's earnest features.

"How can you be so sure?"

"Trust me. I'm sure." Rhoda grunted, bringing her knee up to meet her chin, since her chin wouldn't reach her knee.

Allison's stomach knotted like the granny knot at her waist. Rho never had doubts. She had always said she would wait for her man, and when he came along, she'd grab him with both hands and damn the consequences. Allison cursed her own wary nature. Why couldn't she take her chances like Rho? But Jake Tory was no option. They had absolutely nothing in common.

When she raised her head a second time from her knee, Jake stood beside her.

"Here." He raised her to her feet and deftly untied

the granny knot at her waist, then wound the belt from front to back and around again finishing it off with a smooth square knot. Placing both hands on the belt, he pushed it lower on her hips. "Wear it that way." For a moment his hands lingered on her hips.

Beneath the cotton *gi,* Allison's flesh felt branded. She'd heard of it, but never seen it happen—her toes actually curled!

"Thanks," she mumbled, conscious that Jake's hand still rested lightly on her hip. "Next time I can do it myself." She was expert at scarf tying, and she wouldn't be needing the stiff white belt anymore.

Jake nodded and returned to Kim.

"Will everyone please do as I do?" Jake placed his hands on his upper thighs, his right fist clenched in his left palm and bowed to Kim. Kim returned the bow. "We show respect to our *sensei* in this manner," Jake said. "In this case, Kim or I will be your *sensei,* or teacher, even though you are only studying self-defense, and not the higher forms of karate."

Everyone copied Jake's instructions and waited to be shown what to do next—everyone except Ross, who remained upright, his arms folded defiantly across his chest.

Jake ignored Curran and looked at Allison. "Ready?"

"Yesss!" she hissed, lifting one knee high, arms raised and wrists bent in her best imitation of a karate stance. *Laugh and the world laughs with you, McKay!* Suddenly, her ankle wobbled and gave way, collapsing her into Jake. *Damn!* She'd almost made it without klutzing.

"Crippled Crane defense?" Jake asked, his lips compressed, but his eyes twinkling with humor.

Allison shrugged, sending Jake a sheepish grin. *Crippled crane! Not a swan, or even a goose.* Did she look like a crippled crane to Jake? But why worry now? He'd already seen the real, green chenille Allison with the marshmallow toes. How could he possibly have any illusions about her? Besides, he probably gave those come-hither looks to all his female students.

Jake moved over to correct the stance of the woman standing next to Allison. He issued clear, concise instructions, but he never touched the woman nor retied her miserable knot. Allison felt a rush of triumph. Jake had singled her out, even if it was only for belt tying instruction.

For the rest of the session, Allison tried to duplicate Jake's moves, even though every muscle in her body felt like she was on a torture rack. After class, Rhoda joined Allison in the dressing room.

"Well?" Rhoda nudged Allison's arm.

"Well what?"

Rhoda placed herself squarely in front of Allison. "You said you'd tell me about Jake moving into 3B later. This is later."

"There's really nothing much to tell," Allison said, wishing now she'd kept her mouth shut. "He moved into the apartment next to mine last week. Remember I told you about the inconsiderate kid blasting his boom box? That turned out to be him." She went on to tell Rho about meeting Jake, leaving out the part about the kiss.

"I wish Kim lived next door to me," Rhoda sighed. "He could play his stereo as loud as he wanted. He told me he lives here at the dojang." Rhoda dropped her *gi* on the floor and laced on her sneakers, then tried to jam her feet through the legs of her jump suit with them on.

Finished dressing, Allison prepared to leave. Rho was deep in conversation with Kim Joon. Jake stood in his office door.

"Got a minute?" He stepped back and gestured toward the chair she'd occupied before.

Allison limped to the chair and sat down. Her muscles had already begun to stiffen.

"I've decided to offer private lessons," Jake said. "Perhaps you would be interested—since we live so close to each other. It would put you way ahead of the class."

Allison resisted the urge to massage her aching calves. Who else had he offered these lessons to? She had no intention of being part of a herd of women panting to spend time with the handsome karate instructor. On the other hand, he probably wanted to because she so obviously needed extra help.

Private lessons?

Suddenly, her mouth took another U-turn from her brain.

"How often do you give these private lessons?" God! She really had been kidnapped by aliens and now they were using her voice to communicate. Nothing else could explain this madness. *More lessons with Jake Tory—and alone?* She must be out of her mind. She didn't have time for private lessons.

"As often as you—anyone wants." Jake's lips twitched with the hint of a smile, hoping she would say yes.

At a slight sound behind her, Allison turned to find Kim Joon leaning against the office door.

"I didn't know you had decided to give private lessons—this year," Kim amended as soon as he caught Jake's look. Kim made a slight bow, then turned away, though not quickly enough to hide an enormous grin.

Jake walked over and closed the door. Then, as though Kim hadn't interrupted, he continued. "It's important to be able to defend yourself without weapons." He needed to impress this truth on Allison, and not entirely because of the conversation he'd had with Boswell Graham. He really didn't want her to be helpless against an attacker.

He returned to his seat.

"Later, if you decide to really study tae kwon do, I will teach you."

And who's going to teach me to defend myself against you? Allison thought wryly, knowing it was far too late for that. She'd fallen under Jake Tory's spell the moment she'd first seen him performing his *kata* in 3B. He was the most compelling, gorgeous man she'd ever seen.

"Have you offered this option to the others?" Allison jerked a thumb toward the door where her fellow students were filing out. She sounded prickly, but he'd caught her off guard with his offer of private lessons. Down deep, she'd hoped he'd say she was different from the rest—that she was the only one he'd asked—that no one else would be offered private lessons—but why should he do that? After all, business was business.

"No other private students—just now," Jake said enigmatically. Graham had asked him to arm Allison

McKay against whatever might come of their investigation of Ross Curran. But an inner voice told him how very much he wanted to do this.

Allison scrubbed her soles against the chair rung, glad she now had the protection of sneakers.

"It wouldn't be fair for me to take your time when you could devote yourself to someone who seriously intends to study karate." She was ashamed of the nasty-nice tone of her voice. "Besides," she said as inspiration struck, "I can't afford private lessons."

Jake's dark eyes seemed to see through her thinly veiled excuses, and he wasn't buying them. He squared the papers on his desk and looked her directly in the eye.

"I haven't offered this 'option,' as you call it, to anyone else and, as for cost, we can worry about that later." Graham would pick up the tab—if Jake chose to charge at all. Right then, he felt like paying Graham for the privilege of being with Allison. He fixed her with a stern look.

"Don't take this lightly, Allison. I'd hate for something to happen to you that could be prevented."

Now I'm Allison? She gazed over her head at the ceiling fan gently thumping in slow circuits.

"Is that why you gave me special instruction today?" She counted the fan blades, avoiding Jake's eyes.

Jake lifted an eyebrow. "Was it special?"

"In a way. You did tie my belt for me, and you didn't tie anyone else's. Was it because you thought I'd never get it right?" She turned on a cocky grin. "I took care of myself long before I ever heard of tae kwon do or karate." *Or Jake Tory.* "What makes you think I can't do it now?" She could see she'd touched a sore spot when Jake frowned.

"I help all my students when they need it," Jake said levelly. Graham had warned him Allison would be stubborn about his instruction, and he'd been right. She had a head like a rock to go with that fiery temper and red hair. He swallowed a smile. It would be nice work softening her up.

Allison sent Jake a sour look. She'd show Jake Tory—and Boz Graham. She would learn this self-defense stuff if it killed her—and belt her uniform with the yellow and gold paisley scarf. She sneaked a palm down to rub her sore thigh. She envisioned herself hobbling along on crutches, sidelined for life. She stifled a laugh. If she kept up these classes, she might become a crippled crane for real.

"About the private lessons," Jake pressed, "will Tuesdays and Thursdays at the apartment and Saturdays here with the group be convenient?"

He'd noticed Ross Curran watching Allison during the earlier demonstration and again today. He didn't know why, but he made a note to find out. The man could be more than a thief—he could be . . . Jake pushed away the memories of nightmare scenes he'd witnessed in Hawaii during previous investigations for private clients.

"I thought Boz only wanted us to learn the basics. He won't blame you if I flunk karate." This was her last chance to weasel out.

"Graham might not care, but I would. I want you to learn." His eyes traced her body from head to foot. "You have the perfect shape for karate. Don't waste it." His eyes continued their survey. He'd never spoken truer words. She was perfect for the discipline—*and perfect for him.*

Allison's heart accelerated like an Indy race car. Meet Jake Tory three times a week? Her heart would never stand it.

"Let's see." She ticked items off on her fingers. "I get home from work around six. Nuke dinner. Quick change. How about seven o'clock every Tuesday and Thursday and here on Saturdays until you decide I'm a deadly weapon?" Her overactive hormones must be running wild again. Why wouldn't her lips say the one sensible word: No!

Three times a week? No way falling in love could be avoided with that kind of exposure. She'd just sealed her own fate.

"We'll discuss deadly weapons some other time. You still have a lot to learn, Allison." For a moment, his eyes lingered on her lips before forcing his attention back to business. "Did your *gi* fit?" He already knew the answer. He'd watched her for the past hour.

"Well enough." Allison looked down at the uniform lying across her tote bag. "Shall I wear this Tuesday when I come?"

Jake nodded.

Allison fished the white sash from the jumble and held it out. "Could I trade this for another color?"

"That may have to wait," he said, drawing a deep breath, until the urge to laugh subsided. "Stick with white for now."

A muscle twitched in Jake's cheek. Her naive remark had struck him somewhere near his heart. Those were the words of a little girl and he'd heard them more than once from his younger students.

Ever since meeting with Graham and seeing Ross

Curran eyeing Allison in class today, Jake couldn't shake a strange sense of urgency. Allison must learn to defend herself—and soon.

Allison grabbed her tote bag, ready to leave.

"Tuesday at seven, then," Allison said, yanking open the door. A small voice in her head nagged: *Don't get involved. After classes are over, the handsome Mr. Tory will move on.*

Jake tossed Allison a casual salute and resumed the task of sorting his enrollment papers. He remained at his desk for a long time, the sight of her hips swaying seductively burned behind his eyelids.

In the parking lot, Allison's white Celica and Rhoda's battered red Taurus were the only two cars left. Rho must still be inside cementing her relationship with Kim.

Allison slammed her bag into the trunk. *Beauty shop!* She'd get a jazz cut, close to the head, sleek, trouble-free—perfect for karate lessons. She ruffled her shoulder-length hair. She'd been meaning to get rid of this mop for a long time. No more chignons, no more paying extra for long hair at the beauty shop. She fished her cell phone out of her purse and punched in her hairdresser's number.

Five

Allison's stomach fluttered wildly as she stood outside the door to 3B for her first private lesson. She was tempted to dash back to her own apartment.

The gaily printed green and gold paisley scarf she'd chosen divided her *gi* in the middle. She'd finished it off in a jaunty designer knot. An examination in the mirror told her that she looked pretty good in a baggy sort of way. And since it was only a few steps to 3B, she'd left her feet bare.

Her knees felt totally unreliable as she raised her hand to knock. Silence. Had Jake forgotten their lesson? She fluffed her fashionable sash, vaguely disappointed. She'd almost backed out, and now she wished she'd been the one to stand him up.

Just as she turned to leave, Jake opened the door.

"What have you done?" The words exploded from Jake's lips.

Allison looked behind her. Had he gone mad?

"You cut your beautiful hair!" he exclaimed, then reined himself immediately. "Come in, Allison," he said gravely, stepping back. "I shouldn't have raised my voice. It's just that your hair . . . surprised me."

"You hate it!" Allison fingered the short locks above her ears. His roar had left her feeling strangely naked and bruised. "It will grow back," she murmured, brushing the bangs off her face. *Why was she even having this discussion?* She would cut her hair whenever and however she felt like it and Jake Tory didn't get a vote. But he had called her hair beautiful.

"Does it look too awful?"

"Never awful, Allison." Jake wanted to touch the delicate bangs that had fallen back on her forehead and kiss her. He hated himself for shouting at her. "What you do with your hair is entirely your business." He held the door for her to enter.

Allison looked around, noticing things she'd missed that first night when she'd been so dazzled by Jake's magnificent body, cutting patterns in the amber glow. The room was still spotlighted in amber, and a scent of sandalwood permeated the air. Glancing down, she saw that the floor was covered with mats similar to those at the dojang. What few pieces of furniture Jake had, if you wanted to call enormous pillows furniture, were designed for sitting on the floor and were stacked in one corner. One mirrored wall reflected their white-garbed figures.

Catching sight of her shorn head, a pang of regret washed over Allison. She stared at her waif-like image in the mirror. Jake had called her long red hair beautiful and now she'd wrecked it. When she'd left the salon, she'd thought it looked sleek and sophisticated. Now, seeing it through Jake's eyes, it just looked . . . chopped off.

She glanced at her wrist, but she'd left her watch at home.

"I'm early," she said, avoiding further discussion of her hair. "Just go on with whatever you were doing. I'll wait." She adjusted the green and gold paisley sash and shoved it down on her hips the way Jake had shown her. Apparently the brouhaha over her hair had kept Jake from noticing her hot new effect.

"I'm finished," Jake said, stepping closer. "In time, I hope you will appreciate meditation, too."

With every word, he shortened the distance between them, until he reached for her waist, and for a moment, Allison thought he would take her in his arms. Instead, he slowly unwound the scarf from her waist and laid it aside. Reaching into a small lacquered cabinet, he handed her a white belt, indicating that she put it on.

"Sit down, please. I will explain respect for the uniform and the degrees of martial arts belts at some other time, but first, meditation."

Jake folded effortlessly to the floor and pointed to a place beside him on the mat. When Allison tried to copy him, both her knees creaked.

"You don't exercise often, do you?" Jake observed, seeming perfectly comfortable with his ankles resting on his thighs.

Allison shook her head. "Never. I hate . . . that is, I don't . . . not very often." Her knees were killing her, but she tried to keep the agony from showing on her face as she struggled to emulate Jake's lotus position.

"Close your eyes, Allison. Imagine there is a third eye in the center of your forehead," Jake said softly. "See nothing but through that eye. Rest the backs of your hands on your knees, palms inward with thumb and middle finger forming a circle. Empty your mind."

Jake's hypnotic tone lulled Allison, making her forget the painful discomfort in her legs. She'd only had two days to recover from the last assault on her muscles. Tonight would either cure her or kill her.

She tried to imagine a third eye, but she saw nothing behind her closed lids but an image of the dark-eyed instructor speaking soothingly beside her. Gradually, she forgot about the discomfort in her legs and drifted into a kind of sleep state. She had no idea how much time had passed when she became aware of strong fingers kneading her neck.

"Relax," Jake whispered. His breath brushed her ear. "Empty your mind." She felt a feather touch in the center of her forehead.

"Mmm." Allison rolled her neck and stretched. She didn't want Jake's hands to stop. How did he manage this delicious effect? Why did he even bother? She'd told him up front she would never be a hard-body type . . . but this meditation had possibilities.

When she could no longer stand the sensual massage of his hands, she opened her eyes. Slowly, the scent of sandalwood returned, bringing with it an awareness of the exquisite pain in her knees. Instantly, the spell dissolved. It took both hands to unlock her ankles from where they rested on top of her thighs.

Jake lifted her in strong arms and held her upright until she steadied. Surrounded by the exotic aura of incense, bathed in amber light, Allison wanted Jake to keep on holding her. His hands against her were warmly sensual. At this rate, she'd never make it through private lessons, much less the coming six weeks Boz had contracted for.

Jake released her and stepped away. He couldn't take advantage of her in such a situation. If he could do as he wished, he'd pick her up, carry her to his bedroom and make love to her all night long.

"Ready?"

"Ready," Allison gulped. She felt like a toddler gazing worshipfully up at her instructor, waiting to receive a gold star if she did well.

For the next hour, Jake took Allison through a simple *kata* exercise, working on her balance and flexibility. Soon, he promised, he would teach her a more advanced exercise. But none of this would be practiced in Saturday's class. This was for her alone.

By the end of the session, Allison was exhausted. Jake had forced muscles into action that she hadn't known existed.

"Thursday we will discuss methods of attack and their countermoves," he told her. "If there's time, we'll get into the history of tae kwon do. But first, we have to get you in good physical condition. Do you jog?" He remembered the jogging suit she'd worn to Saturday's class.

"Not really." Allison heard her stomach rumble and felt a twinge of embarrassment. Of course she didn't jog. Only masochists jogged, and besides, she was ravenously hungry. "Have you eaten? I could order Mexican—"

"I've got a better idea," Jake said, taking her hand and leading her to the door. "Shower and change, and I'll introduce you to my favorite sushi bar. It's much healthier."

Healthy—ugh! "I love sushi!" Allison gushed. The aliens were at it again. The only sushi she'd ever seen was dried out on a cocktail tray and she wouldn't have touched it with a pair of tongs. I'm a pathetic liar, she thought disgustedly—but dinner with Jake would be worth all the eels or squid or whatever else she had to choke down.

"Good. Then I'll knock on your door in half an hour. And by the way, try this." He handed her a jar of Tiger Balm. "Rub this into your muscles after you shower. You'll feel better." He itched to apply the balm himself. Perhaps another time. He stepped back. "You won't need much time to fix your hair and I think you can find a better use for this." He handed her back her paisley scarf.

Jake's remark about her hair stoked Allison's temper again. So what if he hated what she'd done to it? And he hadn't appreciated her scarf, either. She snapped the scarf at him, ineffectively, and stalked down the hall. Stiff-arming the door to 3A, she headed for the shower, kicking her *gi* into the air as she went.

Tiger Balm? Sushi?

Six

The sushi bar was a small place located five blocks from the apartment. Wrought iron tables and chairs were scattered haphazardly about, and paper lanterns shaded the lightbulbs. Unfamiliar but tantalizing aromas filled the air and instead of the reedy Asian music Allison had expected, she was surprised to hear the soothing voice of Lionel Richie singing the oldie, "Lady." Why hadn't she noticed this place before? Probably because sushi was the last item on her menu from hell.

Jake selected a table away from the speakers, and held out a chair for Allison.

An older woman came from behind the counter, speaking in rapid-fire Korean. Jake answered warmly in the same dialect. Smiling and nodding, the woman filled plates and brought them to the table.

"This is Mama Chang, Allison. Mama Chang, this is Allison McKay." Jake clasped the older woman's hand and drew her down beside him. "Mama has looked after Kim and me ever since we came to Houston."

Allison nodded, uncertain what to say. Did the lady speak English?

Mama Chang satisfied Allison's curiosity immediately.

"My grandson, Jimmy, work Jake's dojang," she said haltingly, then left to greet new customers.

Jake selected three varieties of sushi from the dish Mama Chang had brought and slid them onto Allison's plate.

"California rolls—even sushi haters like 'em," he announced, lifting one and popping it into his mouth.

"How did you know I was really a sushi hater?" she inquired.

"Your expression." Jake grinned.

Allison inspected the rings of vinegared rice molded around swirls of avocado and cream cheese. An almond sliver was artfully placed in the center of each ring and the whole was bound by a ribbon of green vegetable-like material the menu identified as seaweed.

She lifted a piece of sushi in her fingers and took a bite. The delicious creamy center melted on her tongue. For a junk food junkie, she discovered she liked Jake's sushi. She reached for another morsel of a different type, but the instant it touched her tongue she knew she'd made a mistake. Gagging, she looked for a place to get rid of it without Jake noticing.

An artificial ficus tree sat in the corner beside their table, and when Jake went for more sushi, Allison dumped the unwanted bite beneath its leaves.

"You needn't eat the sushi if you don't care for it," Jake said, returning with chopsticks and placing a pair by her plate.

"I learned to use chopsticks in college," Allison

offered, watching Jake deftly lift the sushi to his mouth.

"College where?" It was the first really personal question he had asked.

"University of Texas—Austin." Allison remembered the take-out Chinese dinners she'd shared with her roommate during exam week. She had learned to use chopsticks on a five-dollar bet that she couldn't afford to lose at the time. "And you?" Allison asked, lifting her chopsticks to scout out another California roll.

"University of Hawaii. My father was assigned to the Environmental Agency at Oahu until he died in a helicopter crash. My mother died when I was born. Kim's parents died in Korea when he was ten. We grew up together in Honolulu in the home of Kim's uncle—who is also our *sensei.*" Jake reached across and adjusted Allison's grip on her chopsticks, pointing them toward the sushi she liked. He'd told her more about himself than he had ever told anyone.

"How did you get hooked up with this Graham Insurance self-defense program?" Allison asked, trying to ignore the tingling in her hand where Jake's fingers had rested. Was it her imagination or had they lingered a second longer than necessary?

"Graham seems concerned that more and more employees are refusing to work in dangerous areas."

"I would never quit my job because of street crime. After all, where would you run?"

"You might not run, but you could stand and fight if you knew how," Jake said. "That's my job—to show you how to stand and fight." He ducked his head to hide a grin. Allison McKay had a long way to go before that beautiful, soft body of hers became a fighting machine. "You do very well with those chopsticks."

"Then, why did you change the way I hold them?" Allison brandished the crossed wooden sticks playfully like tweezers about to close on Jake's nose.

"I wanted to touch you." He stilled her hand, placing her chopsticks on the table.

"Oh," Allison murmured. Jake's straightforward answer made her feel like a teenager on a first date. She'd never met a man she couldn't handle—but then she'd never met anyone like Jake Tory.

Jake's seemingly innocent touch had shattered her resolve. Her vow to stick strictly to business teetered on the edge, ready to fall into the abyss. All she heard was Jake's rich baritone across the table.

She drew patterns with her chopsticks on the table. She was a crackling mass of nerves, and it was time Jake Tory did something about it.

"Boz looks after his people like a mother hen," Allison said. She couldn't manage another bite, and she'd completely run out of small talk.

"Mr. Graham said he was already working with the Houston Police on another matter. That's where he first met Kim and me."

Allison studied the man across from her. Boz must trust this man. But could she?

He lifted a questioning brow and gestured toward the almost empty sushi plate.

"No more for me, thanks." Allison stared openly, fascinated by his soft, almost caressing manner, his long tanned fingers. His simplest moves were beautiful to watch.

Jake toyed with his chopsticks. He wished he could think of a suave way to tell her how incredibly attractive she was. Here he was, faced with a gorgeous redhead he wanted to make love to, and he didn't have a clue how to go about it.

"I've never given much thought to personal attack," Allison said. "I always assume bad things happen to the other guy."

A shadow crossed Jake's eyes. "I believe they call that the Pollyanna Syndrome, Allison. Don't make light of the danger. I'd hate to see anything happen to you."

"Honestly!" Allison threw her hands up and gazed out at the passing traffic. "I'm not cut out for this self-defense stuff. It might be fine for some, but I never leave home without my .38 automatic." She patted her purse beneath the napkin in her lap. "I'd be terrified with only my hands and feet for defense. I have a gun permit and I've had marksmanship classes. That's enough." Why tell him she'd be too terrified to use the gun on anyone, and often forgot to take it with her—like now.

The muscles in Jake's jaw tensed. "Listen to me, Allison. You *can* learn self-defense. Get rid of that gun!" He was overstepping his bounds, but she had to listen. He stilled, reminding himself: *The master of karate is master of himself.*

Allison bristled. "Is that an order?"

"A request, Allison—a most sincere request." His dark eyes locked with hers. "Just a request," he added more softly, gently stroking the backs of her hands with his thumbs.

Jake finished his sushi in silence. From time to time, Allison considered the possibility that he was still angry, but his expression remained unreadable.

He felt her eyes on him.

"If I have to," he said at last, "I'll keep you under twenty-four hour surveillance to make sure you don't shoot yourself with that pistol." He was only half joking. He happened to be doing just that—only Allison didn't know it.

Allison lifted a skeptical brow. "Twenty-four hours a day? And just how would you do that? Put a glass against the wall and listen in on my apartment like they do in old Laurel and Hardy movies?" Grinning, she lifted an empty water glass and placed its bottom against her ear.

Jake pursed his lips. "I'll consider it."

Scooting his chair back, he hitched around to face her.

"Ross Curran," he said abruptly. "The tall, slender guy in my Saturday class—did you know he watches you?"

Allison shook her head. She hadn't realized Jake had seen Ross staring.

"What is he to you, Allison?" Jake asked bluntly.

"Nothing. I went out with him once and lived to regret it. He's a user, Jake. Or maybe it's the other way around—I'm a sucker. There's no reason for Ross to watch me." Her lips twisted wryly. "If there's a mirror around, Ross is usually looking at himself."

She wasn't catty by nature, but all her anger and resentment toward Ross had slipped past her guard.

"That 'once' with Ross wasn't nice, was it?" Jake asked. A wave of jealousy—something he'd never experienced—rippled through him. The thought of that man touching Allison made him furious.

For an instant, angry hurt flickered in Allison's eyes before she shuttered them against Jake's sharp observation. "With all the students in the room, I'm surprised you even noticed him."

"I'm trained to notice, and the sooner you learn to watch your back when I'm not around, the better off you'll be."

"When you aren't around?" Allison's breath caught. "You can't devote every waking moment to me." The more she thought about it, the more certain she was that Boz was behind Jake's intense interest in her whereabouts and companions.

Jake looked down to hide a sudden flare of desire. At that moment, he wanted Allison with a fierceness he hadn't believed possible. Suddenly, Ross Curran had become more than an assignment—he'd become Jake's enemy.

Allison scanned Jake's tense features. Why should he make sure she knew how to defend herself—unless Boz had arranged it? But if she became involved with Jake, she would be risking a heartache that might never heal.

"Ross won't hurt me," she said, gazing at the passing traffic. "He might annoy me, but he wouldn't actually harm me. When you thought you saw him looking at me, he was probably just looking around for his next victim." Allison bit her lip. She hadn't meant to say "victim." It sounded too ominous.

Another couple entered the sushi shop and took a table nearby. Jake watched idly as they ordered, seeming willing to let the problem of Ross Curran drop for the time being. After a moment, he pushed his plate away and extended his hand.

"Come." He dropped some bills on the table and anchored them with a soy sauce bottle. "I'll walk you home."

Allison started to protest that tonight was her idea and she would cover the tab, but something in Jake's expression told her not to try it. Jake waved at Mama Chang, then wrapped a broad palm around Allison's arm and propelled her to the sidewalk.

Traffic hummed softly along Corinth Street as headlights flashed intermittently, illuminating the street scene. Visions of the warm glow in Jake's apartment and his stimulating *kata* exercise lingered in Allison's thoughts. She detected the same spicy sandalwood scent she'd noticed when Jake had returned her keys, and later in 3B. He seemed so rock-solid safe. But was he really?

A burst of noise from a nearby theater signaled the last show had just let out. Jake guided Allison through the throng collecting on the corner. Tightening his grip on her arm, he took a cautious look behind. From the moment they left the sushi shop, he knew someone was following them. A wave of anger seized him.

He stopped walking and drew Allison against him. Whoever had been there was gone. Probably just a panhandler who found fatter pickings in the theater crowd—but Jake couldn't shake the uncomfortable feeling. He continued their walk with slow, measured steps. If the watcher chose to keep up, he would make it easy.

In the final block before reaching the apartment, Jake stopped beneath a street lamp and again drew Allison close for another look behind them. This time, he gave in to a maddening need to feel the softness of her mouth under his. He tried to tell himself this was just a momentary distraction, but the argument failed. He lowered his head and kissed her softly, relieved when she didn't draw away. He lengthened the kiss, no longer trying to tell himself he wouldn't have Allison—tonight.

"You really guard your back, don't you?" Jake whispered. "You weren't even aware we were being followed."

"Are you serious?" Allison wrenched her head around to look. "Why would anyone do that?" Then it struck her. He'd kissed her only to see who was following them.

Jake pulled her close again, struggling against the laughter that threatened to erupt. Her abrupt look behind them would have scared off the most inept tail.

Allison felt Jake's chest and shoulders shake beneath her cheek. Shrugging out of his arms, she turned an angry face upward. "Why are you laughing at me?"

He released a deep-throated roar of laughter. He hadn't really laughed in years and it felt so good. Allison McKay had done things to him that no enemy ever could. She'd made him forget his rigid discipline—not once, but twice.

"No!" he managed to gasp between gales of laughter. "Not *at* you. Just at the whole ridiculous situation." His hard-won control had broken down and the world hadn't ended after all. Concealing emotion from the enemy might be essential—but Allison wasn't his enemy.

"Why would anyone follow us?"

"I don't know," Jake murmured, his lips barely moving as he swallowed another urge to laugh. With Allison craning around, their shadow had to know they were on to him—if there'd ever been a shadow.

"I think we're clear—and I apologize for embarrassing you." His expression was solemn. "But promise you'll keep your doors locked. Walk to your car with other employees from now on. And call me if you need me." He didn't want to frighten her, but she needed to be at least a little afraid.

Gazing at Allison's upturned face, Jake felt his heart turn over. She was so brave, so self-assured . . . and so unaware of the potential danger she was up against.

Allison's eyes drifted the length of Jake's smoothly-muscled frame. It seemed so natural for him to hold her, kiss her. But his urgency alarmed her. He really *believed* they were being followed.

"Surely you don't think—"

"I don't know which of us is being followed," Jake answered honestly. "Someone has been back there dodging in and out of doorways, but he's gone now."

"But why would anyone follow either of us?"

"That's what I'd like to know." Jake resisted the urge to look back once more. Was he carrying this whole thing too far? Since meeting Allison, his concentration had been fractured. Should he relieve her mind and tell her their shadow might be only a panhandler—even if he didn't believe that himself?

He bent his head and kissed Allison again, but now he took his time, molding her against him, fitting his mouth to hers. How could he convince her to give up this idea that she was bulletproof? How could he convince her that learning self-defense was a woman's best protection?

When Jake broke the kiss, Allison whispered sheepishly, "People are looking at us. I feel like we're on center stage at the Alley Theater." She'd never been one to give a real big whup what other people thought, but with Jake, she wanted to keep it private—just for themselves.

"I'm sorry, Allison. Kissing you was the only way I could think of to look behind us without alerting whoever is back there. Besides, I like it." *Liar!* He could have found a dozen ways to look behind them without kissing her. He could have dropped his wallet, or stopped to tie a shoe, a dozen ways, but he'd been greedy. He wanted to kiss her and keep on kissing her, until she begged for mercy.

Allison was shocked at her intense response to Jake's kiss and to the way he'd ruined everything by apologizing. For the space of a heartbeat, his kiss had made her forget every promise she'd ever made to herself about men. Bathed in the glow of the streetlight, his firm jaw set, he reminded her of a warrior tensed for battle. Still, the level-headed side of her argued with her heart. *Sooner or later, he'll disappoint you. Better to keep your distance.*

Jake nudged Allison to continue their easy amble toward the apartment.

"Mad?"

"No. Yes!" She felt the urge to land one on him for that apology. She struck out with a fist, but an instant before it landed, Jake caught her hand, stopping the blow in midflight.

He stared down at Allison's livid face. "What—"

"Arrgh!" Allison growled, struggling furiously. She'd show him mad! Not for the kiss but for all the things he made her feel. Forming another fist, she went for his face, but Jake captured her other hand easily and banded both of her arms to her sides in a steely grip.

"What's this about?" He held her trembling body against him.

"I'm sick of—the way you act so aloof—the way you boss me around—just everything." Her sudden tears drenched Jake's shirtfront. Shuddering, she drew a ragged breath, wanting to condemn him for everything she could think of. "You kissed me for the worst reason—just so you could look behind us, and then you say you're sorry and ask me if I'm mad? Damn you, Jake Tory." She didn't care if people had begun to stare.

"Stop it!" Jake commanded. "You aren't making sense." He looked down at her tear-stained face. "If you're insulted because I kissed you . . . I've apologized. What else can I do?"

Allison drew away. *Men!* Her anger had begun to dissipate, and she was appalled at her behavior. She'd thrown a childish tantrum. So what if Jake hadn't really wanted to kiss her? She had wanted him to want to kiss her.

"Under other circumstances, I might like to kiss you for no reason at all," Jake said, a faint smile lifting his lips, "but you don't seem to believe the potential dangers out there." He didn't want to mention Ross Curran again—unless he had to.

"Doom and gloom. Spare me." Allison dragged her fingers through her cropped hair. If Jake ever kissed her again, it would probably be because a truck was bearing down on them and he needed her for a rearview mirror. "I've lived in Houston all my life. I know my way around. I don't need a bodyguard—or a relationship."

"What about that Curran guy?"

"Dammit!" Allison whirled on Jake, eyes blazing. "I've told you! Ross is less than nothing to me!"

"But does he believe that?" Jake asked softly. "If he wanted to take up where he left off, would you go?"

"Never! I'd go to the devil first." Wrenching free, she headed for the corner.

And I'd fight the devil for you, Jake thought.

Allison stopped to let Jake catch up. "Please, can we just drop this now? For the last time, Ross is history."

"I trust you, Allison, but I don't trust him," Jake snapped, his eyes darkening. "Believe me, Curran's not through with you yet. If he comes near you, I want to know." He would know whether Allison told him or not.

"Really, Jake! We work for the same company. I can't help running into Ross in the course of a business day. But he isn't dangerous."

Jake grasped her shoulders. "Lock up when we get home." He considered for a moment. "Do you have a burglar lock on your balcony door?"

"Of course I have a lock on the balcony door." She couldn't remember if she did or not. She rarely opened the damned thing. "Anyway, you live right next door. I'll pound on the wall if I need you."

"And how would I get in?" Jake asked, amusement in his voice.

"You could huff and puff," Allison suggested with a grudging smile. She pictured Jake's powerful legs smashing the door down. If he wanted in, he'd get in, and he knew it.

"Stop it, Allison," Jake said, gently. "Don't joke. Most doors are pitifully easy to break down." She seemed determined to overrule every precaution he suggested. Whether she knew it or not, she needed him—and instead of saying the things he really wanted to say, he was discussing door security! Why couldn't he just tell her he found her irresistible—that she was destroying his concentration and lowering his defenses—defenses they both might need?

At the final traffic light before they reached the apartment, they halted to allow a stream of cars to pass. A young boy was hawking newspapers on the corner. Jake bought one and stuck it under his arm. Across the street, a tired-looking woman sat on a camp chair offering single roses for sale. Jake bought one for Allison and handed it to her with a slight bow.

Allison lifted the blossom to her nose. She wanted to get home and think, far away from Jake Tory. If he did one more lovable thing like give her a rose, she'd cave in and invite him to stay over—and not on the sofa.

Jake's silence lasted until they stopped in front of 3A.

"Go home, Jake, I'll be fine," Allison said brightly. "And thanks for caring."

Jake studied her determined features. Her insecurity showed plainly. A sudden flood of words rose up in him and spilled out.

"I've never met anyone like you, Allison—never wanted to protect someone so much from the least thing that could harm them. I know," he raised a palm, "you don't need anyone, but you do—you need me." He finished on a softer note.

Raking his fingers through his hair, Jake paced a short distance and returned. "Why are you making it so hard for me?" His jaw muscles rippled from the effort not to say more. "I want to make love to you—and you want me to. Admit it."

Hard for him! Allison covered her eyes with both hands, conscious of a gentle breeze lifting the wispy ends of her cropped hair as she fought to regain her composure. *He's never met anyone like me. Is that good or bad?* The humid Houston air had become tropical, settling thickly around the city. The steady hum of traffic three floors below blended with the exciting vibrations racing through Allison's body. She wanted to reach out to Jake, touch him. Feel his hard body surrounding hers, sending its fire through her, warming her, protecting her. *Loving her.*

Damn Jake and his discipline! Why couldn't he be devious like other men? Why couldn't he give her some reason to hate him—to exclude him from her life? She wanted to ask him in, but she couldn't allow this to happen. If he ever made love to her, she'd be lost—but if he didn't, she'd still be lost.

Bitter arguments flew back and forth inside her head. This man towering over her so still, waiting, could be the love she'd hoped for all her life—but she couldn't risk it.

"Goodnight, Jake," Allison said at last. When she looked up, she saw a flicker of disappointment in his dark eyes, but he didn't try to stop her when she slipped through the door and closed it behind her.

Inside, Allison rested her forehead against the smooth wood paneling.

"Go away, Jake," she whispered, bleakly. "Please. Go away."

Seven

Monday morning traffic was as snarled as a rag picker's sweater.

Allison drummed impatiently on the steering wheel, sipping coffee from her to-go cup, glancing morosely at the drivers closest to her. Not a smile among them and she was no better.

Boz had asked her to meet him early. He seemed certain Ross was about to make his move.

Although there was still close to a million dollars missing, no new fire claims had come through, and she couldn't stall any longer. Sooner or later, she'd have to face Ross and tell him she'd blow the whistle on him, if he didn't hand over half the money. She'd given that a lot of thought—maybe too much thought—but he had to agree to take her with him. How else could she find out where, and in which bank, he'd stashed the money?

A chilling thought struck, causing her nearly to ram the car next to her. *If Ross kills me, there'll be no one to challenge his charges against me. I'll be buried under the tombstone of a thief.* And he'd be out of the country. The creep was as cautious as a prairie coyote when it came to protecting himself . . . but if she could show him the benefits of taking her along, he might consider it a good way to stay out of the headlines.

Allison gulped cold coffee, her mind working furiously. She'd left home an hour early to keep Jake from following her. The mere thought of going anywhere with Ross made her stomach churn, but at the moment her stomach churned from lack of food.

A bicycle messenger zipped between cars and whacked her fender, then flipped her the bird. Allison sent a long blast on the horn after him.

"Face it, McKay," she groused. "You can't back out now." Her job put her at the very hub of the scam. But why couldn't Ross have picked someone else to snooker into his dirty plan? Like Herb Miller—he handled the final payment affidavits, stamped them with the company seal. Why had Boz ruled out Herb as a suspect? Or had he?

Traffic inched another half block, until Allison was able to turn down the ramp to her reserved space in Graham Tower's underground garage. The moment she got out, an eerie feeling swept over her. Was she imagining it, or were there fewer lights in the parking area this morning? She wished now that Jake was with her as her footsteps echoed hollowly through the chilly, oil-tainted atmosphere to the elevator. She resisted the urge to look over her shoulder.

On the main floor, the elegant marble lobby was deserted. Then footsteps approached.

"Good morning, Allie. You're in early."

Allison whirled to see Ross Curran emerge from the coffee shop just off the lobby, his sharply handsome features wreathed in a patronizing smile.

"Morning, Ross." Allison forced something that felt more like a grimace than a smile. "Why so early?"

Ross had avoided her at work all week, and now he was here at the crack of dawn. Did he know about her meeting with Boz? But how could he know? She was letting Jake's warnings get to her. Under the harsh neon lights of the coffee shop, Ross no longer seemed sinister in his finely tailored Brooks Brothers suit—but he did look tense.

The familiar marble floors and columns in the twenty-year-old building took on a funereal atmosphere. She was alone in this vast echoing place—with Ross Curran. The small hairs on her nape lifted. She couldn't escape, short of knocking the man down and running for her life.

Ross had gripped her elbow and was edging her toward the garage exit when the soft ding of the elevator door opening made him turn. Allison pulled away as Boz Graham stepped out and came toward them.

"Mornin', folks." Boz nodded somewhere between the two of them. "We're an early crew, I see." He paused beside Allison with his back to Ross and mouthed, "Later."

"How are the self-defense classes coming along?" he asked Allison.

Ross shouldered in front of her.

"Waste of money, Boz. By the time you go through all the bowing, a determined mugger will knock you flat—if he doesn't knife you first." Ross shot his cuffs and straightened his regimental striped tie. A smug smile twisted his lips.

"Bear up, old man," Boz said negligently. "Set an example for the 'little people' you always talk about." He turned and headed for the coffee shop.

Ross stiffened. With his artificial smile still in place, he hurried after Boz.

Allison wished she knew even one karate move, but with her luck, she'd miss and fall on her face. She felt a little foolish, but she couldn't entirely dismiss the idea that Ross might be the one stalking her. Why else would he show up here so early and for no apparent reason when he never had before—unless he'd followed her from home? She'd read somewhere that criminals got paranoid when they were about to be caught.

How simple it would be for him to follow me here, silence me, then let the public assume I was just another mugging victim.

Allison released a ragged breath. She'd been standing there as though she had an iron bar welded to her spine. She cast a last glance at the two men in the coffee shop. She'd pass up a freshly-baked cinnamon roll rather than spend another minute around Ross Curran.

Savoring a last spicy whiff, Allison entered the elevator. As the doors slowly closed, she saw Ross prattling away while Boz nodded occasionally and continued reading his newspaper.

When she entered her office, Allison found a stack of pending files waiting. Clipped to the top file was a memo from one of her Betty Boop notepads, in Boz's handwriting, asking where he could get some notepads like hers. Allison grinned. Boz had just solved her Christmas present dilemma. She would put a personalized pad of Betty Boop notes in the huge reindeer sock the employees pinned to Boz's door every year.

If only all her problems could be solved that easily.

From now on, she would take every move Ross made seriously. She was convinced now that Ross *had* followed her to work, just so he could threaten her—or worse. If Boz Graham hadn't showed up . . . She'd just opened the first file when the phone rang. It was Jake. Even angry, his deep voice sent a thrill racing through her.

"You didn't wait for me. I thought we'd agreed—"

"We didn't agree on anything," Allison cut in. Even though she was pretty certain she'd fallen in love with Jake, she wouldn't hand her life over to him. But his voice resonating through the receiver set up a bittersweet ache in her heart—and lower. Why did she run from something she wanted more than anything? Easy. Because, one day Jake might move on and she couldn't face that.

"I've got a lot of work to get through, Jake. If I come in an hour early every day, I just might be able to see the top of my desk by Christmas." And maybe by then Ross would be in jail and she could get on with her life.

She kicked the wastebasket beneath the desk and felt better. Jake's protectiveness drove her nuts. She felt like a fugitive running from Ross and Jake, two very different men, both monitoring her every move.

"Let's have lunch. I'll come for you at noon." It wasn't a request.

"Can't. Too busy." Allison bit her lip, she wanted to say yes. She was starving, not just for food, but for Jake.

"Can and will," Jake said, briskly. "Noon." He hung up before Allison could answer.

It hadn't mattered to him whether she said yes or no. What was happening to her? No man had ever taken over her life the way Jake Tory had—and to make matters worse, she loved the way it made her feel. For the first time ever, someone seemed to care what happened to her.

"Ready?" Jake stuck his head through the office doorway at noon. He'd walked the few blocks to Allison's office.

"I told you I didn't have time for lunch." Allison still had to see Boz sometime today.

Jake's eyes were fixed on the picture tacked to the door.

"You're a Harrison Ford fan, too?"

"He's my secret lover," Allison said flippantly. She saw a momentary flicker of surprise in Jake's eyes. If he only knew her secret fantasies about *him.* "Sit down, Jake and let's get something straight. You have to get over the idea that you can tell me what to do and when to do it. I did very well before I met you, and I'm perfectly capable of deciding when, whether, and with whom I'll have lunch."

Jake withdrew into silence for a moment.

"Sorry, Allison," Jake said at last. "I didn't realize you felt so strongly. If you don't want to have lunch with me, I'll leave." He stood just as Ross pushed through the door and skidded to a halt at the sight of him.

"Socializing on company time, Allie?"

"You'll have to excuse me, Ross, Jake and I are going to lunch." Allison carefully closed the top file on her desk.

When Ross started to reach for the file, Jake stepped between him and Allison. Ross stepped back.

"I just dropped by to see if you needed help with those claims," Ross said, gesturing toward the closed files. "If you want me, just call. After all—I owe you one." With an icy stare, he stepped into the hall, pulling the door shut behind him. Allison shivered. *His help? Owe me one?* She slammed her lap drawer and fumbled for her purse. She wanted to stomp the cold-blooded creep into the carpet. He'd seen Jake come in, and wanted to stir up trouble—unless he was after something in those files on her desk. She made a note to check them thoroughly after lunch for anything missing.

Jake slipped an arm around Allison's waist.

"Why did you leave without me? What is it you aren't telling me?" Jake demanded.

"What makes you think I'm holding back?" If Jake only knew about yesterday's bus incident . . .

She'd been on her way to meet Rhoda for lunch. She was delayed at a crowded bus stop waiting for the light to change.

Rho had gone on ahead to grab a table for them. Though New York Deli was just across the street from Graham Tower, Allison balked at the idea of walking even that far in the midday heat.

A bus had just lumbered off, leaving a trail of exhaust fumes. Allison covered her nose, waiting for the *Walk* sign to flash on. She dabbed a handkerchief to her neck, idly reading the T-shirt on the large woman in front of her: "I'M A SENIOR CITIZEN. GIVE ME MY DAMN DISCOUNT!" Another bus was on its way down the block. Allison looked despairingly at the *Walk* sign. Was the damn thing broken?

She edged to the curb, ready to bolt the minute the light changed. Then someone jostled her from behind, hurling her into the street, directly in the path of the oncoming bus.

"Hey! Watch it!" The T-shirt lady grabbed her arm, pulling her back. "You better look out, honey. That bus is a lot bigger than you are!"

As soon as the light changed, the woman hurried across the street.

For a moment, Allison simply stared at the enormous bus chugging off down the street. Her heart beat an irregular tattoo, and her mind raced wildly with "what ifs." What if she'd been killed or horribly maimed? But she hadn't stumbled off the curb. She'd been pushed!

Ignoring traffic, Rho skipped back across the street to Allison. She'd seen the whole thing—except for who had pushed her.

"No foul, no fault," Allison quipped.

"You didn't trip this time, Allison," Rhoda said gravely. "Someone pushed you. I saw you lurch forward. Did you get a look at the people behind you?"

"Why should anyone push me? You're talking as if someone's out to get me. I don't matter that much in the scheme of things." Allison didn't feel good about shutting Rho out this way, but her best friend couldn't keep a secret to save her life.

"Some people don't need a reason," Rhoda said. "They just do awful things in faceless crowds." Rhoda's soft brown eyes narrowed. "You do realize you've had more than your usual quota of accidents lately, and don't try to blame it on being a klutz."

"Thanks for the compliment," Allison said, grinning. She'd tried to convince herself it was just her own clumsiness, but she *had* felt that palm in the center of her back. . . .

She brought herself back to the present moment.
"Let's go while we still have time for lunch," she said, shouldering her purse. Over Jake's protests, Allison insisted on driving them. "Never walk when you can ride and never ride when you can fly," she told Jake airily, swinging up to the drive-through window of a nearby taco stand.

Eight

Jake's desktop was littered with junk food.

Allison munched contentedly on her burrito while Jake took microscopic bites from a taco she'd bought for him.

A smile hovered at the corner of Jake's mouth. He loved Allison's joyous approach to life, her obvious love of food that was pure poison to him, her loyalty to her friend Rhoda, so many things he'd never known in a woman, combined to make his redheaded beauty irresistible. Despite his carefully acquired discipline, he was trying to eat a taco when all he wanted to do was hold her and kiss her.

Boz Graham had assured Jake that he knew Allison was innocent, but he was still willing to take a chance by using her as a decoy. She could be hurt, or even killed, playing Graham's game.

Jake leaned forward, bracing for another bite of taco.

"Watch your papers. You'll get grease all over them." Allison scooted a file out of the way with her elbow and took a practiced bite from the monstrous rolled tortilla in her hand. She looked guiltily at Jake. The beef and refried bean filling stuck in her throat. She felt foolish stoking down grease bombs while Jake scarcely ate a bite. A feeling of warmth filled her. At least he'd tried. Jake wrapped his mostly untouched taco in a napkin and tossed it in the sack.

Allison grinned. "You don't like your taco, do you?" she asked, all innocence.

"A rhetorical question, I assume," Jake said, disdaining an answer. "By the way, my partner Kim has been seeing Rhoda on a regular basis." He shoved his chair back and propped his feet on the desk, placing his hands behind his head. "Did she tell you?"

Allison frowned. She'd known from the first day in the rec room that Rho was attracted to Kim, but her friend hadn't mentioned they were dating. She set her burrito on the paper.

"Rhoda always said she'd shop until she found her man. Apparently she has."

"Apparently." Jake's tone was caressing. "And how about you?"

Allison sent him an enigmatic smile, continuing to munch her burrito.

Jake straightened and shoved the greasy taco sack farther away.

"Sushi after your lesson?" he asked, enjoying Allison's barely concealed shudder.

"Why not eat at my place? I'll run by the deli and pick up sandwich makings." Maybe she'd stop by Mama Chang's and ask what sushi Jake liked best and bring some home for him. Suddenly, the idea of Jake "home" for dinner filled Allison's mind with plans: she would light the rose candles, drag out her unused dinner plates and wineglasses—just for Jake. And . . .

"Allison! Over here!" Jake pointed both index fingers at his chest. "Am I boring you?"

"No way! I mean, no! Of course not." She held

her burrito up like a talisman. She'd broken her own rule by allowing Jake too close. Now she was asking him to an intimate dinner—with wine.

"Sorry I'm not such good company," Jake said, rounding the desk to stop beside her chair. "Maybe this is better." He took the burrito from her and took each of her fingers in his mouth to suck it clean, then folded it into her palm. "There. No more greasy fingers. Try to cut down on your poison intake, will you?"

With each sensuous flick of Jake's tongue, heat flared in Allison's stomach. Did he have any idea how sexy he was? Did he know his every move, every gesture made her want him?

"Really, Jake, I've managed my diet very well all these years. Trust me when I tell you Tex-Mex food doesn't kill." She tried to steady her voice. "Once you pass phase one, I'll introduce you to jalapeño peppers." Did he know how his "intake of poison" had left her weak? Was he trying to drive her nuts on purpose?

"I'll eat jalapeños, if you'll learn to love sushi."

Allison grimaced. How could such a beautiful man eat such disgusting food?

Jake grinned at Allison's disgruntled expression. "Are those jalapeño peppers a threat or a promise?" he asked. In Honolulu, he'd eaten habañero peppers with raw fish quite often.

For a moment their eyes locked. The fire blazing between them was hotter than the salsa that came with the tacos—hotter than a sidewalk in July—hotter than. . . . Allison felt dizzy from the sensation of Jake's body leaning over her. He kissed her lightly, then lifted her onto his lap.

"Save your self-defense for class. Don't use it on me," he murmured against her lips. Holding her close, he traced feathery kisses up the column of her throat, stopping for a slow, toe-curling kiss against the shell of her ear.

"Ja . . . ke," Allison drew out his name with a sigh. The velvety touch of his tongue on her fingers had sent shivers of desire racing through her, and now that roving, tantalizing tongue left her limp and breathless.

She buried her fingers in his hair, tugging his face down.

All she could feel was Jake's hard body pressed against hers, his growing arousal beneath her thighs, and all she could hear was a fierce rush of blood in her ears. He kissed her again, slowly, their mouths mating as though made for each other.

Somewhere inside, a tiny voice nibbled at the edge of Allison's consciousness. *I can't do this.*

Jake's belly tightened. He'd never felt such an overwhelming desire for a woman. Until now, life had been austerity—discipline—then this funny, sweet woman had come into his life with her cropped red hair and those long, luscious legs. At least the legs were still there and her short haircut would grow out, he thought ruefully. Allison had taught him to laugh. She had evoked emotions he'd never known he possessed.

From the moment he'd caught Allison McKay in his arms at the karate demonstration, he'd wanted her. He wanted to take her with him into the silent places, keep her safe, make love to her.

"Sensei?" Jimmy Chang stuck his head around the doorframe.

Allison leaped up guiltily, straightening her emerald linen dress, and smoothing down her tousled hair.

Jake rose slowly, gently urging Allison back into her chair. He seemed totally unaffected by their brief, passionate kisses, and not in the least upset by the youngster's intrusion.

"You need me, Jimmy?"

"Yes, *sensei.* Your afternoon class is gathered."

Mama Chang's grandson took his duties very seriously. His dark eyes had shown no surprise at the sight of his *sensei* holding a woman on his lap. An unwelcome thought occurred to Allison: did Jake entertain other women in his office this way?

Allison slipped into her shoes.

"Go on, Jake. Take your class. I have to get back to work." She had to meet Boz later. Her breathing was still ragged, and she doubted her knees would support her. But Jake just stood there calmly. Thank God Jimmy had come in, or they would have ended up making love on the desk, right in the middle of the taco carnage. Jake's gaze was full of promise as he followed her to the door.

"Wait. I'll go with you," he said, slipping his feet into the loafers he'd kicked under his desk. "Kim can start the class." He couldn't leave her alone. Those were Boz Graham's orders—and his own wish.

"No need!" Allison protested. "Go! Your class is waiting. I've got the car." She gathered up the remains of their meal and tossed them in a wastebasket outside the door. Boz would be expecting her right after lunch—and she needed time to think about what had just happened with Jake.

After a moment's hesitation, Jake went to the closet

to get his *gi.* As he passed, he dropped a kiss on Allison's lips and another on his way back to the door.

"Go straight to the office—and lock your car doors," he said. "I'll see you tonight." He headed for the dojang.

Tonight? She'd invited him for dinner after class *tomorrow* night. Rho would be over tonight for her weekly ice cream orgy. But Jake had definitely said "tonight." She checked her dress again for telltale wrinkles. Did he think her dinner invitation was a pitch to go to bed? Well, what if it was? What had just happened made it hard to pretend that Jake had no place in her life. Allison released an uneven breath. Why not take her chances? But she was afraid.

All afternoon, Allison fought daydreams about a life with Jake. She grinned at the idea of her handsome karate instructor coming home from a hard day at the dojang to stuff himself on sushi, while she would sit on his lap munching a Snickers bar. But her fantasies were seriously interfering with her work. She kept feeling Jake's lips gently sucking her fingers, his tongue tracing the pads, his kisses brushing her face like butterfly wings. Jake Tory was everything she'd sworn to avoid: handsome, forceful, sexy, everything a man should be.

How could she bear it if, when their classes were over, Jake walked away? What if he had another life outside karate? Allison wondered. *As if that would change anything.* He'd worked his own brand of magic on her from the first. Would it be so awful to make love just once? If she were to take the risk, she wondered if she would be able to let him go.

Her meeting with Boz after lunch had been short. He'd told her he had additional information, and knew that Ross had recently purchased airline tickets for two passengers, paying cash, and leaving the destination and date of departure open. According to Boz, she was the only one who could discover Ross's ultimate destination—where he'd stashed the embezzled money, and under what name. She had to convince Ross of the advantages of taking her with him—and sharing the loot.

Allison lifted the phone and buzzed Ross's extension.

"Sorry I ran out on you at lunch. Was there something you wanted?" She bit her tongue to keep the sarcasm out of her voice.

"We can't talk on the phone. Why don't I drop by your place? We can discuss . . . things," Ross was like a feral wolf, alert, wary. Did he sense something might jeopardize his getaway?

"I'm tied up tonight and tomorrow, and I have a lesson Thursday. How about Friday?"

"Friday's not good," he said. "Can't you cancel whatever it is you're doing and see me tonight?" He sounded edgy and impatient.

"Not possible," Allison said. "Friday."

"I'll let you know." Ross hung up as though someone had just entered his office.

Allison sat for a minute, digesting Ross's strange behavior. His tone was urgent. Was he in such a big hurry to silence her? Should she cancel with Jake for tonight? Ross might bail out *before* Friday—before she had a chance to pitch her deal to him.

Allison released a gusty breath. It would be tough, but she had the scene she planned to play with Ross all blocked out in her head. She would work on his vanity, using greed as her motive the way Boz had suggested. She'd tell him the prospect of sudden wealth had proved to be an unexpected turn-on. With his conceitedness, it just might work.

If Ross didn't contact her by morning, she'd go to his office, drop all pretense and lay it out for him: she wanted a share of the loot and a ticket out of the country if she was to take the blame for stealing it.

After dismissing his class, Jake joined Kim in his living quarters at the rear of the dojang. Kim cooked his meals in a small electric wok he kept in a low cabinet against the wall, and slept on a futon similar to the one in Jake's apartment. Kim preferred living in the austerity of a dojang as he had during his early training.

Kim moved to his improvised kitchen, and returned with a bottle of plum wine and two small cups. Jake recognized Kim's signal that he wanted to talk.

Handing Jake a cup of wine, Kim sank down on a cushion, and grasped his own cup in the traditional manner, fingers flat beneath the bottom, thumb steadying on the rim. His brows were dark slashes above his grave, almond-shaped eyes as he contemplated Jake. With nothing to restrain it, Kim's straight black hair fell nearly to his shoulders. He shook it back with a practiced swing of his head. In Jake's opinion, Kim was a classic example of an aristocratic Korean. And there was more to their closeness than mere friendship. They shared the sacred bond of Zen.

Kim took a sip of wine and set his cup aside.

"We need to talk about this Graham assignment. I've been tailing Curran, and you've stuck to Allison." Kim smiled wickedly. "Would you like to trade?"

"Not a chance, friend."

"Am I right? You would stick close to her whether on assignment or not?" Kim's white teeth flashed in a playful grin.

Jake merely smiled and took another sip of plum wine.

"That brings us to Rho. I've been seeing her often—and I hope I'll be seeing her for the rest of my life," Kim confessed.

Jake raised up from the cushion he leaned against. "That serious? I knew you were dating, but—you love her?"

"More than I thought possible," Kim said, not the least self-conscious.

Watching his closest friend bare his heart, Jake knew he hadn't been honest with himself—or with Allison. He'd fallen in love with her and hadn't told her. That old wariness of his—that law-of-the-jungle alertness so essential to a master of martial arts—had spilled over into his private life.

"Strange, isn't it," Jake said. "We both met women we could love."

Kim refilled Jake's cup. "Have you told Allison?"

"Not yet. But I plan to when this Curran business is over—she won't give it up!"

"That's a cop-out. Tell her, Jake."

"How can you be so sure we'll live through this assignment?" Jake asked. "And how do you know Curran won't try to kill Allison when he no longer needs her?"

"I *don't* know. But as long as I have one day with Rho, it's enough to last me to the end of my life."

"Brave man, Kim. I wish I were more like you." Jake released a breath. "Maybe you're right. I haven't been fair to either of us."

"You're afraid you may have to kill Curran, aren't you?"

Jake gave a sardonic laugh. "We both know that Boz wouldn't mind, so long as he gets his company's money back."

Kim reached for the wine carafe.

"Have a little more wine, Jake, and promise me you won't freak!"

"You sound more like Rhoda every day. I won't 'freak.' What's on your mind?"

"Captain Heslip at the Houston Police Department told me that an anonymous informant says we're using the dojang as a front for dealing drugs."

"What?" Jake exploded. "Why didn't you tell me?"

"I *am* telling you," Kim said, calmly. "You said you wouldn't freak, so listen. Heslip says he knows the tip was phony. What he doesn't know is who would want to do this. Any ideas?"

"Curran. But why? He's got all the cover he needs."

"Allison," Kim said succinctly. "Ross doesn't like the way she looks at you. I've been observing him in class. He probably figures he can get at you through her, and get at her by hurting you. It's pure spite."

"But he'll need some sort of evidence. The police can't arrest anyone on an anonymous tip—"

"Curran knows as well as anyone that even if we're cleared, all people ever remember are the charges, never the vindication." Kim refilled both small cups with plum wine. "Let's go on the assumption that the police will have to investigate."

"I suppose you're right." Jake leaned back. "What have you got on Curran so far?"

Kim referred to a small notebook.

"His usual routine is to arrive at work at nine in the morning, work until noon, lunch at an exclusive men's club. If he's lucky that day, one of the women in the office will take him home for a quickie."

"Did Rho tell you that?"

Kim grinned, but didn't answer the question. "As I was saying: Curran detours by the bank, but only to make a routine deposit. Captain Heslip has arranged with the bank to alert me if Curran makes any sizable deposits." Kim referred to his notes again. "Then he goes to dinner, usually in the company of the blonde of the week, then home to her place for the night. This is what needs checking out: I've watched the various women's apartments. There are times when Curran leaves in the early morning hours, but he's lost me every time." Kim's features clouded. "This guy's no amateur, Jake."

"You think he's meeting someone else—someone who's *really* heading the operation?"

"What do you think?"

"It's possible. I've sensed Allison is being followed, but I've never been able to confirm it. If you're onto Curran, you'd know if he followed us the night we ate at Mama Chang's, wouldn't you?"

"He didn't."

"Then who?" Jake swallowed the last of his wine.

"It could be someone assigned to keep tabs on tae kwon do masters." Kim frowned, not buying his own assumption. "I'd almost forgotten that could happen when the discipline is practiced outside of Korea. But surely Uncle Hajimi knows we'd never be involved in the drug trade."

"I wish I knew what the tipster told the police—and if he told anyone else."

"I need to contact Heslip—ask him to get in touch with Uncle Hajimi and have him ask if we're being watched by Korean government men because of our rank."

"Do that." Jake set his cup aside. "You say Heslip knows the informant's charges are false. Would he be willing to call our *sensei?*"

"I've already asked him, and he agreed." Kim offered more wine, but Jake shook his head.

"I told Allison I would see her tonight."

Kim grinned and set his own cup aside.

"Rho's going over to Allison's for an ice cream social tonight. Which means unlimited quantities of gossip and Blue Bell's best. They'll probably stay in the apartment, and you'll be right next door all the time. The ladies will be perfectly safe," Kim told Jake.

"But Allison's expecting me for dinner—"

"Rho said tomorrow, not tonight. You're so transparent, Jake. Try to get through one night without Allison—I'm having to spare Rhoda, too. There's time to tell her you love her."

Jake grinned sheepishly. "Do you think Allison sees through me as easily as you do?"

"Only if you want her to." Kim laughed, tossing Jake a small salute.

Nine

Allison had just stepped out of the shower and slipped into her robe when the door bell rang. She'd left work a few minutes early to get ready for Jake and their candlelight dinner.

"Jake?" There was no answer. Whoever was there had stepped to one side of the peephole.

Was he playing games? Hastily wrapping a towel around her hair, Allison wrenched open the door.

"Hello, Allie." Ross Curran glanced past her through the door to scan the room.

"What are you doing here, Ross?" Allison tried to close the door, but Ross blocked it.

"No need to rouse the building." His glance slid toward 3B.

"I'm getting ready to go out. I thought we agreed to meet Friday."

"*We* didn't agree on anything." Ross's face was a mask. "Ask me in, Allie."

"Some other time. I told you I was going out." She tried to hide her growing panic.

"I'm coming in." Ross shouldered his way into the living room, kicking the door shut behind him.

"If it's business, we could get together tomorrow over lunch. Right now you'll have to excuse me."

Allison reached for the doorknob, but Ross pressed his hand against the door.

"We have some unfinished business, Allie. Business we can conduct without your karate man."

Allison stepped back and clasped her arms across her chest.

"I can't think of anything we haven't already said."

"You seem so tense lately, Allie dear. I thought we'd buried the hatchet."

I wish. In your back.

"Why me, Ross?" Allison asked coldly. "There are plenty of eager women you could have conned into doing your work."

He shrugged. "But I needed your signature on those fire claims to get them through the system unnoticed. You're the final sign-off before claims are stamped for payment."

"What do you mean 'through the system'?" Her chest tightened. She knew exactly what he meant, but she wanted to keep him talking, until Jake showed up. She was alone with a ruthless man—a thief who might not hesitate to kill her.

She scrubbed her damp palms against the rough surface of her robe, glancing sideways toward 3B. Jake wouldn't be home yet, and she needed him desperately.

Ross's tall frame blocked the door. His immaculate business suit and stiff white collar seemed so normal, but Ross was anything but normal.

"Are you really so naive, Allie? Didn't you notice that every claim you signed paid damages to a brand new policyholder? That's right." Ross sent her a triumphant smile. "Those new policyholders were me"— he jabbed a thumb at his chest—"and the fire claims were arsons that I arranged."

"Boz will find out. We'll never get away with it." Allison hated the quaver in her voice.

"We? You mean you. I don't intend to leave a scrap of evidence pointing to me. I have your signature on those releases. Sweet little Allison, guilty of arson, fraud, theft. Mmm. What else can I think of?" He laughed nastily. "Think about it, Allie. There's nothing to indicate my involvement, and everything to indicate yours."

"You could never make that charge stick. With my testimony, the police will investigate you, too." She slid a glance toward 3B. "It looks like you've got things pretty well nailed down," she said, circling Ross to get nearer to the door. "Since it looks like I'm going to get the name, I want in on the game." She leaned against the table in the foyer. "Look, wouldn't it be easier if we disappear together? If I stay, it will be all over the newspapers, and when I implicate you, the chase will begin. If nothing else, I can make you a material witness to *my* crime."

Ross turned and locked the door.

Now Allison was really afraid. There was no back door, and the patio terrace was too far away—and double locked.

"That's better," Ross said. His handsome face altered in a nasty grin. He followed when she backed away. "You're all mine now, Allie. Body and soul—and bum rap." He thrust his face near hers. "You'll do whatever I tell you to, or you'll go to jail."

Allison twisted furiously. If she could just reach her gun—but it was safely tucked away in a drawer at Jake's suggestion.

She threw back her head to scream, but her attempt was cut short by a hand over her mouth. She fought for breath. This couldn't be happening.

Ross Curran, the suavely urbane department store dummy, had become a common mugger.

"How would you like to be the star of a kidnapping, Allie? Beautiful redhead found dead—all the usual?" Ross's laugh grated harshly on Allison's already overtaxed nerves. "Well, it's about to happen. We're getting out of here."

Allison's stomach lurched. In another moment she would vomit. *Oh, God!* Why couldn't she remember at least one simple karate move Jake had taught her? But Ross was too clever to get within her reach. She wrenched her head to one side to scream, but Ross smothered her mouth with his palm again. With his other hand, he delivered a powerful slap to her face. She fell heavily against the leg of the sofa. He bent to strike her again when a tremendous crash sent the door flying off its hinges.

Ross wrenched toward the sound. Jake dragged him away from Allison and hurled him against the shattered door frame. Holding Ross upright with one hand, Jake bent his knuckles to deliver a lethal blow, then stopped.

"I can't kill you, Curran, but nothing can stop me from beating you to within an inch of your life."

"No, Jake," Allison screamed, "he's not worth going to jail for. Just get him out of here." She had to explain to Jake what Ross could do to her—tell him why his attempt on her couldn't be made known.

"Not this time, Allison," Jake growled, landing another blow that broke Ross's nose.

"Not my face!" Ross screamed, wriggling in Jake's

grasp like a bug stuck on a thorn. Jake held him suspended on tiptoe. Cocking his head to one side, he calmly watched the blood flow from Curran's nose.

"Please, Jake," Allison begged, holding her hand over the red handprint on her face. "Just get rid of him. Please?"

Jake hesitated. The sight of Allison covering the place where Curran had hit her, and the terror in her eyes, rekindled the urge to mete out immediate punishment. Every trace of discipline had deserted him. He wanted to kill Ross Curran.

"I'll let you go this time, Curran, but if you come near Allison again, you're dead."

To kill was against every precept Jake had lived by and believed in, but a primal impulse stronger than a lifetime of training had come unleashed when he'd seen Allison helpless on the floor.

"Let him go, Jake. Please," Allison said softly.

Jake continued his hold for a moment longer, torn between releasing Ross or ruining his pretty face permanently.

Hatred glinted from Ross's slitted eyes. Jake knew if he released the man, he'd only return to strike again—like a snake. He drew Ross's face close to his.

"I'll be right behind you, Curran. Remember that. Every step you take, I'll be there."

Lifting the beaten man, Jake dragged him through the shattered door. Like a sack of garbage that had escaped its container, he kicked Ross down the fire stairs, one step at a time. He'd come close—so very close to murder.

"How badly are you hurt?" Jake asked, returning to place an arm around Allison. With one finger, he lightly traced her cheeks, before gathering her to him like a broken doll.

"I'll be all right," Allison sniffled, dabbing at her nose. She snatched another tissue from a box on the end table, scrubbing her lips, still remembering the hideous feel of Ross's steely grip on her arms and his suffocating palm across her mouth.

Allison's tears finally subsided into soft, hiccupping sobs.

Jake lifted her and carried her to the bedroom. A livid bruise was already forming on her cheek.

"He was going to kidnap me," she whispered. "He wanted to silence me—by force, if necessary. I never got a chance to tell him—"

"Tell him what, Allison?"

"Ross is beyond dangerous, Jake, he's crazy."

"Tell him what?" Jake repeated.

Allison sighed. "You may as well know. Boz wanted me to approach Ross with a demand for part of the loot, since he was setting me up to take the blame for his crimes. Then I was supposed to offer to go with him, so I could discover where he was going to locate the rest of the millions he's stolen." She blew her nose and winced. "Boz said the police would be at the airport to head Ross off before he could take me away. The missing piece of the puzzle is where Ross hid the money."

Jake's lips drew into a thin line. "How could Graham put you in such a dangerous position? He hired me to guard you . . . but he didn't tell me he'd asked you to go with Curran."

Allison gazed at Jake, aghast. "Hired you? He never told me . . ." That was why Jake had stayed so close to her. But he hadn't been assigned to kiss her—or make her love him.

"It seems there are lots of things Graham never told either of us," Jake said grimly.

Allison laid her head wearily on Jake's shoulder. She couldn't be angry. After all, he'd tried to protect her.

"What happens next? Do you think Ross will go to work with his face in that condition?"

"He'll have to," Jake said, his jaw clenched tightly. "We're all in a conspiracy of silence now. He knows you won't tell Graham what happened here. From Curran's standpoint, the prospect of money should keep you quiet." Jake dropped a gentle kiss on Allison's uninjured cheek. "We're back to square one. Now Ross will change his departure schedule, since he failed to grab you today."

Jake's eyes narrowed. "You said Ross came to silence you. Do you mean kill you?"

Allison felt Jake's muscles gathering beneath her palm. "I don't know why I said that. I just meant he wanted me to quit screaming."

If Jake knew everything, he'd kill Ross, despite her pleas. She wouldn't let him sacrifice himself for her. She would deal with Ross on her own.

Allison studied Jake for a moment. She already cared for him so much, but she'd brought him nothing but trouble.

"That's a hell of a bruise. Let's get some ice on it. Then I'm taking you to a doctor."

"Wait!" Allison stopped him. "There's something I have to tell you."

"Tell me later," Jake said. "You need attention. Are you hurt—anywhere else—besides your face?" he asked, unwilling to ask how far Ross had gotten with his sudden attack.

"No. You came before he could drag me to his car."

Jake nodded and headed toward the kitchen.

"Just let me take care of you, okay?" he said, stifling a wild array of emotions. He wanted to safeguard her, love her, take her away with him. Fury ran through him at the thought of Curran's hands on her—and the danger she was in. Her life was worth infinitely more than the missing millions, but she didn't seem to think so, for reasons Jake didn't understand.

"Please, Jake. Sit down. Let me explain something." She drew a deep breath. "Since I'm the only one who can find out where Curran hid the money, I promised Boz I'd get to the bottom of this somehow."

"Allison, you can't do it alone. I won't let you."

"That's not your decision, Jake."

Jake swallowed. A wave of tender protectiveness filled him. Under all that bravado, Allison was scared stiff. And if she thought for one minute that he was going to let her catch this creep by herself—armed with nothing but that paisley scarf and a pistol she probably didn't even know how to use—well, she'd better think again.

"Let me back you up, then. At least trust me enough to tell me everything that happens from now on."

A grimace that was meant to be a smile twisted the side of Allison's face that Curran had slapped. "I do trust you, Jake. I never thought I would, but I do."

"Well, that's a start," Jake said dubiously.

Taking pity on Jake's confusion, she went on.

"From the first, I sensed you were different. You didn't come on to me the way other men did. In fact," she sighed, "I was afraid you weren't even interested in me—and I wanted you to be."

"What? You're not making sense, Allison." Yet her words stirred emotions that swirled inside him like a summer storm. He felt as though he'd just come away from a full-contact karate match. "Can we talk about this later?" A lot of strange, wonderful feelings rocketed inside him, changing too rapidly to be absorbed all at once. "I'm going to make you an ice pack."

Allison lay still listening to the clink of ice cubes from the kitchen. Had she scared him off?

Then it was time to change the subject.

"How did you know I was in trouble?" Allison called out.

Jake returned to lean on the doorframe, a whisper of a smile at one corner of his mouth.

"I held an empty glass against the wall the way you showed me."

"Well done!" Allison managed a crooked smile. "Now tell me. How did you *really* know?"

Jake shrugged. "I saw Ross's car in the underground garage when I came in, and I knew there was only one place he'd be heading. When I reached our floor, I heard scuffling, and you know the rest."

Allison reached for a scrap of humor. "You didn't huff and puff the way you were supposed to, you just kicked the door down."

"It's my specialty," Jake said, grinning. He was relieved that Allison could joke again. She'd taught him to smile, to laugh—to love. The thought hit him with staggering force. Discipline had nothing to do with love. Hiding one's emotion in combat was essential. Even so, he'd lost it and revealed his killing rage to Ross. But Allison was not his enemy—she was the love he'd never expected to find.

Jake laid ice wrapped in a towel against Allison's cheek.

"I was so scared," she groaned. "I couldn't remember a single defensive move you taught me."

"Don't worry about it now," Jake whispered, grasping her icy fingers. "Even the simplest karate moves take time and practice. The first rule to learn is self-confidence. You don't trust yourself enough—yet. Relax now. I'm here." He stroked the short hair that spiked around her face like a fiery halo.

Allison sighed and settled against Jake's chest. He lifted Allison into the curve of his shoulder, watching her eyelids flutter closed. He had to find a way to make Curran move up his scheduled departure before Allison got any more involved. He wanted to be the one to take Curran down himself.

Guilt stabbed his conscience at the sight of Allison's bruise. After all his precautions, he hadn't been here soon enough to protect her when she'd needed him. An inner voice reminded him once more that a master of karate was master of himself. But Jake knew the next time he came near Curran, he might not be able to stop himself from killing him. He'd already allowed himself to beat a man who didn't stand a chance against him. He couldn't betray a lifetime of discipline again.

Suddenly, he knew exactly what to do.

If he could carry out his plan, Boz Graham would no longer need Allison for a decoy to find the missing millions.

Jake held her until she fell asleep. Then he carried her gently to her bed, and went back into the living room to call Kim.

Ten

Allison groped for the edge of the bed, and her hand encountered Jake's solid frame beside her. Still groggy with sleep, she raised her head. The ice pack Jake had changed in the night had turned liquid and warm next to her pillow, but much of the swelling on her cheek had subsided.

She slipped a hand over Jake's heart, feeling its steady beat. His closed eyes were ringed with dark shadows. A glance in the dressing table mirror across from the bed told her she looked like hell. She had to do something to make herself look human before she left for work.

Jake stirred and reached for her, drawing her into the curve of his body.

"Good morning," she sighed, allowing him to hold her a moment longer. "Thank you for staying." She hated having him see her look like this.

"Did you think I wouldn't?" Jake kissed her softly. "Wish I could make that disappear," he said, gently brushing a kiss across her cheek but avoiding the bruise.

"Me, too," Allison groaned, trying to laugh, but it still hurt to smile.

"I love you, Jake," she whispered. "I swore I'd never say that, but it's true. I do."

Jake remained silent so long, Allison feared he was searching for a way to let her down easy. Then he cupped her chin in his palm and nudged her hair aside with his bristly cheek. "And I love you, too, Allison," he sighed, planting a kiss against her ear.

He'd actually said the words he thought he never could—and meant them with all his being. He'd waited all his life for Allison. He knew now that he'd only been marking time until the day she'd walked into his life.

Allison leaned up on one elbow and looked into Jake's sleepy eyes. "Make love to me," she whispered.

"You're in no condition for lovemaking," Jake said, rubbing his stubbled chin. "Besides," he argued as much to himself as to her, "there'll be time enough for lovemaking when . . . you're better." He'd almost said, *when this Curran thing is over.* Dropping a kiss at the corner of her lips, he swung his legs over the side of the bed. "But I want to make love to you more than you can imagine." Desire raged through him, challenging every ounce of self-discipline he possessed.

"Please, Jake," Allison pleaded. Her hand crept around his waist, then slipped lower on his abdomen. "Please don't leave me with nothing but the feel of Ross's filthy hands on me. You said you loved me. Prove it."

Jake felt like an animal for wanting her so fiercely. "Are you sure, Allison?" he asked solemnly.

"I've never been surer," she whispered. Then she pulled him down to her . . . and Jake didn't resist.

His lovemaking was sweetly tender. He reined his

hunger, taking care not to rush her. With Allison, he felt open and vulnerable. He was ready to place his soul in her hands. And if this was all they would ever have together . . . he wanted it to be the best sex she ever had. He cradled her in his arms, tracing her body from throat to instep with his lips, drawing her into him—mapping her body—worshiping every inch of her. Allison met him eagerly, clasping his head, raining kisses on his cheeks, careless of his beard. She couldn't get enough of his loving, and all memory of Ross Curran's traumatic attack left her.

Then Jake entered her, and made love to her with a gentle passion that sent her heart spinning into a secret place inhabited by just the two of them. She felt cleansed—renewed. She gloried in Jake's lean, hard body molded to hers. She filled her senses with his own unique scent. When they climaxed simultaneously, she knew, for better or worse, she'd surrendered her life to Jake Tory.

Jake's heart pounded so hard, he thought it would burst. Allison was truly his own to shelter and protect now. He should have found the strength to resist. But his heart was too full. Allison loved him. He loved her. Still, he hadn't been there to protect her—even from himself. He'd been unable to resist the first unreserved lovemaking he'd ever known.

He lay beside her, his hand cupping her breast and looked down at Allison's contented smile. She was sleeping. He gazed tenderly at her dozing features, memorizing everything about her. Even with the bruise on her cheek, she radiated an inner beauty. She'd given him a peace he'd never found, and he knew he would carry this feeling of oneness with her for the rest of his life.

Allison stretched luxuriously beneath Jake's hand. Then they made love again, and though her bruise still hurt, the joy of Jake's touch eased away the pain. Through all her lonely years, she hadn't believed there could ever be a Jake. Lots of men had tried their luck with her, but none had ever reached her heart.

Afterward, Jake lay quietly, but his thoughts tumbled. Whatever it took, he'd have Allison in his life. She had taught him to laugh and love. He wouldn't lose her now.

Jake tucked a lock of hair behind Allison's ear and drew her against him. He remembered how shocked he'd been to see her glorious red mane cropped off. He passed his thumb idly across the silken strands above her ear. Her hair was growing back. He sighed, utterly content.

Jake's gaze moved to the glass panes of the balcony door. It had begun to rain, and he watched the first drops race down the slick surface.

Allison tilted her head upward. There was a sudden sadness in Jake's dark eyes.

"What is it, love?" Was he sorry he'd made love to her? "What?" Allison asked again, rolling onto one elbow to look down into his face.

"I was just admiring my prize," Jake said, lightly, looking away from the window to smile down at her. "Do you know you're very beautiful, Allison?"

"As if!" She attempted a crooked smile, then gave it up when the pain made her wince. "I look like road kill," she joked, trying to tease Jake out of his somber mood.

Jake lifted her fingers to his lips. "There's more to you than beauty, Allison. I love your stubbornness, your determination to take care of yourself—your bravery. I'm just lucky no one has carried you away before I could." He dropped a soft kiss on her lips. "You're not alone any more, love."

"No. Now that I have you," she whispered.

Now all he had to do was convince her to let him protect her—whether she wanted him to or not. His lips curved in a slight smile, recalling her stubborn feistiness when she'd first stormed into his apartment. She'd looked bizarre then, too. But beneath it all, he'd seen this beautiful redhead. After a lifetime of damming up his feelings, miraculously, the words he thought he'd never say to anyone had come effortlessly. He'd been able to tell Allison that he loved her—but he would make no long-term commitment—not until Curran was in jail.

If the plan he had in mind worked, he and Kim might force Curran to move up his scheduled departure—as only they knew how to do. Only highly skilled martial artists could enter a place undetected and leave it without a trace. That was what he and Kim must do tonight.

Allison burrowed against Jake, inhaling the spicy scent that she'd associated with him from the moment she'd met him.

"I never knew much about love when I was growing up," she murmured. "I didn't get long with my parents and they didn't think much of me. You know," she held Jake's eye, "you're the first person ever to say you love me." She caught her lower lip in her teeth to still its trembling. "Please don't say you love me if you don't mean it."

"Hey, from the moment I saw you come through my door and give me hell, I think I loved you," Jake chuckled, planting a quick kiss against her temple. As unlikely as it seemed, he actually *had* known from that first instant that Allison McKay was his destiny. "Now stop frowning, or you'll ruin your pretty face."

Allison felt a laugh vibrate low in Jake's chest beneath her ear. "You really *are* a piece of work," he whispered. He wanted to fold her inside him and keep her safe from every bad guy in the world. "I'll love you forever," he murmured into her hair. That much he could promise.

Together they lay watching daylight break through the clouds and Allison fell asleep again.

Rhoda's panic-stricken voice called from outside the hastily patched front door.

"Allison! Let me in! Are you all right?"

A deep rumble followed her shout and Jake knew Kim was with her.

"Hang on, Rho." Jake hurried to the splintered door. "I have to dismantle this thing." He tugged an opening for Kim and Rhoda to squeeze through, and stepped back.

"What's going on?" Rhoda eyed the damage and the blood spatters on the floor. "The message you left for Kim said to get over here fast, but we didn't pick it up until this morning. What's happened to Allison?" Rho headed for the bedroom.

"Wait!" Jake called. "Allison's asleep. Let me fill you in first. You, too, Kim."

Jake told them about Ross's attempted kidnapping, including the beating he'd given the man—and his lack of remorse for doing so.

Kim looked at Jake oddly. "I think, my friend, you

have at last found the balance between discipline and judgment." He clapped Jake on the shoulder. "I think I like this Jake better."

Jake grinned sheepishly, placing a finger to his lips. "Allison needs to rest—"

"Rho? Is that you?" Jake shrugged and made no protest when Rhoda rushed for the bedroom door.

Jake led Kim to a chair in the breakfast room, out of earshot. Straddling another chair, he faced him across the table.

"Thanks for coming, Kim. I'm planning a little breaking-and-entering party—and you're invited."

Jake set forth the details of his plan.

"We have to find out when Curran plans to leave and if possible, what bank is holding the money he's stolen. We have to make sure the police get to him before Allison gets too deeply involved in Graham's scheme. He's using her for a decoy, and I don't like it. We haven't much time left. Are you ready to play ninja tonight?"

"Ninja? Everyone knows there's no such thing as ninjas," Kim sputtered. "So," he chuckled, "who do you want killed?"

Jake laughed sourly. "I could name at least one, but killing isn't what I had in mind." He went on to explain.

Kim grinned eagerly. "I'll dig out our best black pajamas and be ready when you are."

Jake heard Rhoda and Allison's soft voices drifting from the bedroom and held a finger to his lips. "It might be better if they know nothing of this," he said rising. "If Curran is at home tonight, we'll get to practice being invisible."

Jake knew he could be placing Kim in mortal danger, but his partner was the only person who could help carry off a night raid.

"We'll have to get in and out fast," Jake said. "Curran mustn't know anyone has been there, or our bird may take flight too soon—and punish Allison for it."

"No problem," Kim replied.

Jake's eyes on Kim were somber. Together, the two of them were a formidable fighting force—and tonight, they might just have to put their skills to the test.

Eleven

Allison reported late for work, and just as she opened her office door, Ross Curran piled in behind her, his face hideously swollen from Jake's beating. Allison blocked him in at the entry.

"Keep away from me! You've got nerve coming here." Allison examined Ross's distorted features. "And just how do you plan to explain that face of yours?"

"I've taken care of that, Allie dear. I told them I took a fall playing polo over the weekend. You've done a good job of covering up what I did to you." Ross's lips twisted in a caricature of a sneer as he attempted to move around her. "Maybe I didn't smack you hard enough."

She turned her back, wishing now she'd told Jake to call the police. Then her eye fell on the stack of files he carried.

"Haven't you collected enough blackmail material? Take those files and get out." She gestured toward the open door. If he didn't leave, she'd wait in Rho's office until he did.

Allison studied Ross's once-handsome features for a moment. His evil had begun to break through the surface and show. His soul's disfigurement had oozed up from some subterranean hiding place. Was she the only one to see it?

She started to leave, but Ross grabbed her arm roughly.

"Aren't you the least bit curious about these?" He dropped the files on the corner of her desk.

Allison glanced down. The top file was labeled, "Tory-Joon Loan." Wrenching free of his grasp, she flipped open the folder.

"What are you doing with this? Boz handles the insurance reserve loans. You've got no business with them."

"You forget, Allie, I already handle sensitive documents every day. In fact, I can alter the way they read." He stood in the doorway, blocking her exit. "Pay close attention, my girl. If you don't, I'll see that the Tory-Joon loan is called in. That will finish your precious Jake and his Korean buddy. I'll let it be known that I've seen certain things, since I've attended self-defense classes in their dojang. It doesn't take much these days to raise suspicion of drug trafficking. Just a call or two to the local police . . . and Interpol."

"Why am I not surprised?" she sighed. "Of course you'd lie. You're a thief. What's a lie or two more to you?" She tried unsuccessfully to control the quaver in her voice. "Aren't I enough? Why ruin Jake and Kim?" Her look of loathing was lost on him. "Leave them alone. Take your spite out on me."

Ross followed Allison to her desk to lean over her. She felt like she was alone in a dark room with a giant tarantula. A bizarre, off-the-wall thought struck her mind: he was wearing Hermès cologne. The scent had imprinted in her mind ever since his attack.

Her eyes flew to the closed office door. *Please. Somebody come in.* Any other day, Rho would be here, or a dozen other people would drop by, either on business or to chat, but today, she was trapped, alone with him. If she hit the intercom, what would she say? Ross is threatening me? He'd only tell another bland lie.

"Why Jake Tory? The man actually means nothing to me." Ross lifted a hip onto the desk. "But I've been watching you with him. It strikes me that you might be more agreeable to what I have in mind if you thought something might happen to Tory or his karate school." His cold gaze oozed malice. "Maybe a fire in the dojang . . . or just calling their business loan due would be ruinous enough. If you care about the man, Allie, you'd better listen closely to what I have to say."

"You wouldn't dare," Allison gasped. "Boz won't let you do this." She stole another glance at the intercom, clenching her fists until her nails cut tiny half moons into her palms.

"Oh yes, I'd dare. I've made certain you will be charged with those arson frauds," he said, his lips twisting nastily. "You can't deny the signatures on the claims are yours. But I need a little more, ah, insurance." He paced to the door and back. "It's only a matter of time until Graham discovers I've borrowed the company seal from time to time. Before he does, I intend to get away. That's where you come in."

Allison stared, speechless. If Ross could gain access to the company seal, what else might he do? The imprint of that seal on the documents was the main reason the claims were paid.

"How did you—"

"—how did I get the investigator's seal? Simple. I conned Herb Miller the same way I conned you."

The bastard was right. At one time she'd been taken in by his good looks and urbane manner. But since Boz had put his scheme in motion, she'd wised up.

She stared at the ceiling, willing the tears in her eyes not to overflow. Ross had openly confessed to arson and fraud, and set her up to take the rap. Her temper flared. Dammit! He wasn't going to get away with it.

"Keep talking," Allison said, stiffly.

Ross sidled around the desk to stand beside her and thrust his face close to hers. "You can't *prove* your innocence."

Allison could see herself not too long ago, pen in hand, signing every file he put before her, without really looking at them. She remembered how he'd urged her to get done so they could move on to more "enjoyable" things. Once he'd used her loneliness against her—and now he was using her fears for Jake.

His voice dropped to a threatening growl. "I need time to get out of the country, Allison. That's where you come in. Graham will think you signed those claims and collected the four million dollars in payouts—that's why you have to disappear. By the time the investigation leads to me, it will be too late. I'll be—never mind where I'll be."

Allison's stomach plunged like a carnival ride. *Disappear? Disappear as in dead?*

"Four mil . . . don't be ridiculous." She pretended not to know it was so much. "Boz will know it's a lie. He knows I'd never do such a thing!"

"Not if I take you with me when I leave. Listen up.

Here's the scenario: Two lovers run away together with a pile of Graham's money. Everyone knows we went out together. Neat, don't you think?"

"We went out once!"

"All right. Once. But you signed those claims over a long period of time. Think about it, Allie. Think hard." Ross gathered his files, unlocked the door and stepped into the hall.

Allison slumped behind her desk, resting her head in her hands.

By the time she reached home that evening, Allison's nerves crackled like frayed electric wires. Throwing herself on the sofa she stared at the ceiling. Sitting still proved impossible. Pacing the room, she hugged herself in despair. The apartment seemed emptier than ever. None of the cheerful touches she'd surrounded herself with helped. The sofa was the same cheery yellow-and-white stripe, but without Jake's long, beautiful body there, the room was empty as a church on Monday.

When she went into the bedroom, her stuffed seal smiled up at her with his wistful button eyes, and Allison burst into harsh, convulsive sobs. She hugged the furry white toy to her breast, rocking it the way she longed to be held and rocked—the way she longed to hold and rock a child of her own. She might destroy the man she loved, and the only way to keep him safe was to go with Ross and keep him away from Jake—somehow.

A knock on the door roused Allison. When she opened it, Jake leaned against the frame. She should send him away. But doors couldn't keep Jake out—not from her home, nor her heart.

"You're late for your lesson." Jake edged around her into the room. "I heard you come in, then when you didn't show up—" He peered at her closely. "You're trembling . . . sweetheart, you've been crying!" He gathered her in his arms, stroking her back and making soothing sounds against her ear. "If this is about Curran, you know I'll never let that low-life near you again. If you don't want him handled my way, at least let me go to the police."

"No, Jake!" Allison reached up to trace the curve of his firm lips, loving the feel of his muscular shoulders curved around her protectively. She slipped a hand beneath his *gi* to brush her fingers lightly over his nipples, delighting in the shiver she caused. She wanted him to make love to her, at least one more time before . . .

"Ross won't bother me again."

"How can you be so sure of that?"

"I'm sure. Just stay clear of him." Nothing she said would make any sense to Jake. He had nearly killed Ross once. If he knew the plan, he might succeed this time, and ruin his life. "No police," she repeated firmly.

Jake drew her over to the sofa and pulled her down on top of him, grinning up at her.

"Three falls to a finish?" he asked, working on the buttons of her blouse. He didn't want Ross between them just now.

"Best two out of three sounds fair," Allison said, landing a kiss on Jake's nose, then slipping down to capture his lips and draw his tongue into her mouth.

Jake managed to shed the jacket to his *gi* and slip

her blouse off her shoulders. Slipping two fingers beneath her bra, he unfastened the catch, allowing their bare flesh to touch.

"What did I ever do before you?" Jake sighed. "You're all I ever wanted, only I didn't know it until now."

Allison lay still, cherishing the feel of Jake's finely honed body beneath her. She couldn't bear to lose him now.

"It's the same for me. I never knew—"

"Words just get in the way," Jake said, lifting her to remove the rest of her clothing and slip out of his cotton canvas trousers. "Here or in the bedroom. Your call."

"Sofa, floor, ceiling, just so long as you make love to me," Allison whispered, tracing her palm the length of Jake's lean flanks, delighting in the shivers her stroking caused.

"Why not all of them?" Jake grinned, positioning her over him to fit their bodies before driving into her to the hilt.

The thrill of Jake's sudden entry made Allison gasp. Then she began to move, trying to get closer, get more of Jake . . . before she couldn't have him any more.

Lying quietly in Allison's bedroom, their third lovemaking venue, Jake said, "Tell me what's bothering you, love. If it's not Curran, then why are you so set against the police? Curran committed an open-and-shut case of assault, and I'm your witness."

"If you go to the police, Ross will only make liars of us both. You have no idea how clever he can be."

She rested her head in the curve of his shoulder, softly stroking his flat stomach. She had to send him away before Ross destroyed him. "Don't worry about me. I'm fine. I just cleared a heavy workload today, that's all."

"Graham wouldn't mind if you took a day or two off," Jake said, placing a tentative finger on the bruise she'd made up so carefully. "Still hurt?"

Allison shook her head. She hurt from something far deeper than any bruise.

"No days off just now and no Rho to help." She forced a laugh. "Have you forgotten I'm headed for a promotion?" She handed Jake the TV remote and jumped up. "Can I get you something?" she asked with forced brightness. "The usual?" She might be taking more than a few days off soon—for an all-expenses-paid vacation with Ross Curran.

Jake nodded, switching channels without really looking at what was on the screen.

Once out of Jake's sight, Allison leaned against the sink, staring vacantly. She had to organize her thoughts. Make up logical excuses to stop seeing him. But when he was near her, every resolution dissolved.

When she returned with two bottles of spring water, she heard the shower running. Jake stood beneath the spray in all his naked male glory.

"There's room for two," he said, extending a hand.

Allison set the spring water on the basin and stepped in beside him.

Between soaping, laughing and making love again, warm water cascading over their joined bodies, another hour passed before Allison remembered.

"Sorry I was late for my lesson. I guess . . . I forgot." She glanced around for the spring water. "Give me a minute to get my *gi.*"

Wrapping a towel around her hips, she headed for the bedroom. Jake was right on her heels, dripping water with every step. At the door, he swung her back against his water-slick chest.

"You're acting strange, Allison. Tell me what's the matter."

"My karate *is* improving, isn't it?" she said, evasively. His warm breath brushed her nape. Her towel slipped to the floor. She wanted to throw her arms around him and bawl like an infant.

"Listen, Allison," Jake said softly, smoothing a vagrant strand behind her ear. "Ross's attack should prove to you the need to learn self-defense. The man's not through with you yet."

Jake was right. Ross had forced his way into her apartment with ease, and she'd been unable to do anything about it.

She ran her fingers through Jake's hair and pulled his face down to hers, tracing his jawline with kisses. She could still feel Ross's steely grip on her arms and the vicious impact of his slap against her face.

For a long while they just held each other. Then Jake drew away and reached for his *gi.*

"You're not up to a lesson tonight, sweetheart." He passed a thumb gently down the line of her cheek. "I'll stay here with you and drive you to work in the morning. Kim and Rho will be along soon. And yes, your karate is improving"—his lips curved in a half smile—"but not enough."

"You worry too much, Jake." Allison's mind had started functioning again. Anger had become her ally. Whatever it took, she'd protect Jake from Ross.

"Allison?"

"Mm?"

"I love you," Jake said, placing both hands around her throat, and nudging her face up with his thumbs.

For a moment, Allison's heart skipped with hope for a future, then reality flung her back to earth.

"How can you love me? For all I know, this could be over when Curran is caught." She loved this man so very much, it hurt her to hurt him, but she must distance herself from him—now, before it was too late. Her tone was as brittle as broken glass. "I never thought you'd take it so seriously." Allison ached at the sight of Jake's stunned expression.

"Allison, didn't you hear me say I love you? I've never said that to another woman." Jake grasped her shoulders and turned her to him. "I've never loved anyone until now. You love me, too. I know you do. Say it."

His tender words were more than Allison could bear. She broke down, sobbing.

"I can't stand this, Jake. Just go away and leave me alone. Trust me when I say we can't be together." She wrenched from his grasp and ran toward the bathroom.

"Don't run from me, Allison," Jake shouted, catching her and swinging her around. "I'm talking about love. I want to be with you, care for you always." He pulled her into the living room and gently pushed her backward onto the sofa. "Now," he commanded softly, "say you love me." He dropped down on top of her, straddling her hips with his strong legs.

"I want to marry you, Allison," Jake said solemnly. "Now, how's it going to be? Kicking and screaming all the way to the altar or willing and wonderful?" He tugged one of her short curls. "Now say it!"

"Oh God, yes! I love you, Jake—so much." Allison covered her eyes with both hands. "You just can't imagine."

"What can't I imagine?" Jake teased, drawing her hands away from her face.

Allison didn't resist when Jake continued to straddle her. She might as well get this over with. Trying to convince Jake that she no longer wanted him would never work.

"You have to promise that you won't interfere with Boz's plan to trap Ross," she said. "Boz and the police will step in before I'm in danger." Jake had to believe that. If only she could.

"No promises, sweetheart, but let's hear the rest."

An hour later, an exhausted Allison had told Jake Ross's entire scheme, including his plan to take her with him as a hostage. If she didn't go willingly, he would call in the Tory-Joon loan. She didn't mention her fear that Jake would kill Curran.

Emotionally drained, Allison lay quietly in Jake's arms.

"Do you really think I care so much about the loan I'd let you go away with Curran?" he softly inquired. "Boz wouldn't let him call it anyway. You should have told me."

"I didn't tell you because I was afraid you'd . . . do something to upset the police trap."

Jake's expression hardened. "Forget the loan. Kim and I can find financing elsewhere. But if that bastard Curran thinks he's taking you away with him, I'll do more than upset the police trap," Jake fumed, squeezing her so tightly she struggled for breath. "I might have changed his mind permanently—I still might." Jake set her away from him and rose to pace angrily.

Where had his hard-won discipline gone? He felt as though he'd never had it. All those years of meditation, calming the soul, freeing the mind, had deserted him. All Jake wanted to do now was kill the man who was threatening Allison—the woman he loved.

"Listen to me, Jake. I only learned about the loan business this morning. If I'd told you, you would have confronted Ross before I could find out where he's hidden the money he's stolen." Allison dashed tears from her eyes and groped for a tissue. "Please don't try to change my mind, Jake. I'm going through with Boz's scheme. Ross isn't going to get away with it. After all, I'm the one he's blackmailing. But he's going to pay for what he's done, sooner or later."

"Give me time to think this through," Jake said, calmer now. "There's a way out of this and I'll find it." *I'll find it tonight in Curran's apartment,* he vowed silently.

Jake surveyed Allison's stubborn chin, stroking her rigid backbone. She was so proud, so self-confident. She could get herself hurt—or dead, if he didn't keep her out of Curran's hands. This latest threat went far beyond anything he had imagined.

"Just when I have a life, this has to happen," Allison groaned. "You're not going to love me for long if this is the kind of trouble I get you into."

"Allison." Jake placed a gentle kiss against her forehead. "I can handle trouble. But Kim and I may have to go back to Hawaii to explain some things to our *sensei.* Someone called in an anonymous tip to the police here and in Honolulu, charging Kim and me with selling drugs from the dojang."

So Curran had made good a part of his threats already. Allison shuddered.

"How long have you known this? Why go on about how you're going to protect me, if you plan to leave?"

"I don't want to go anywhere until Curran is caught. That's why I wanted to call in the police," Jake said. "Listen to me. I should have done this before."

Jake began to speak softly, explaining that if their *sensei* sent for them, they could only delay so long before they must face him and prove that the drug charges were false.

"Then Kim will be going, too?"

"Yes," Jake said. "Kim is my closest friend. We trained together—and when we took on private investigations during our time in Honolulu, he saved my life more than once. Now my life belongs to him. We both swore a solemn vow never to bring shame to our *sensei* nor to tae kwon do. I must honor that." Jake stared into the distance. "Even without my debt to Kim, I would have to present myself to my teacher. No martial arts master can fail to obey his *sensei's* command." He took both Allison's hands in his. "Kim's in love with Rhoda. He doesn't want to leave her any more than I want to leave you, but an obligation more compelling than you can imagine obliges us to answer to our *sensei*. Do you understand, Allison?"

Allison clasped her arms around Jake as though she could hold his life between her hands—keep him from giving it away—keep him from leaving her.

"I don't really understand, but I have no choice

but to trust you." She trembled in his arms. "Oh, Jake, what are we going to do?"

"Say nothing about this to anyone, Allison," Jake cautioned. "If we can stop Curran, there'll be no scandal and no need for anyone to know anything." And if Jake could get Heslip to back him up, there'd be no need to explain anything to their *sensei.*

But, Allison thought, there might be no more evidence to support Jake's innocence than there was to support hers. Who would believe a smart businesswoman like Allison McKay had been duped into authorizing payment on fire claims without scrutinizing them?

Laying her head against Jake's chest, she listened to his steady heartbeat for what might be the last time. Burrowing her fingers in his hair, she inhaled his essence, imprinting everything about him on her heart and soul and lifted her lips for a kiss.

Tears slipped slowly down her cheeks. Was their love strong enough to survive this?

Twelve

Allison buried herself in the comfortable familiarity of the office routine, filing papers and clearing off her desk. She had just sat down when Rhoda bounced through the door.

"You shouldn't be here. You should be in bed!" Rhoda's eyebrows lifted, making worried lines on her forehead.

"I'm fine. I just want to forget the whole thing." Allison pointed a schoolteacherish finger at Rho. "And I don't want anyone else to know about what happened. Okay?" Deceiving Rho wouldn't be easy. If her best friend knew even half of what Ross planned, she'd confront him without stopping to consider the consequences.

"Allie, you're hiding something, and if you won't tell me, I'll ask Jake." Rhoda reached for Allison's phone.

For a long moment, Allison gazed through the window. Everything seemed so normal outside. Road haze dimmed the skyline, and people moved along on their way to who-knew-where, never guessing at the drama unfolding behind the blank reflecting windows of her office building. She swung back to Rhoda.

"Just how much do you know about Kim and Jake's life before they came here?" she asked at last.

Rhoda looked guiltily at her hands.

"Kim said Jake has some notion that he owes him his life. It's because of something that happened in Hawaii. He and Jake had some problems, but he wouldn't tell me what."

"There's more, and you know it."

Rhoda hesitated, braiding her fingers nervously. With a sigh, she said, "Kim pulled Jake out of some sort of street shoot out and kept him from getting run over by a fleeing car, or something like that." Rho's voice trailed off at Allison's startled look. Jake hadn't mentioned a street fight, or a runaway car, just that Kim had saved his life.

"Hold it! You didn't know any of this, did you, Allie? Damn! I've blown the whistle again."

"I knew some of it," Allison replied, "but I want to know everything." She fixed Rhoda with a piercing stare. "Now talk."

"I've told you all I know. But," Rhoda said, "it seems you've been keeping quiet about an awful lot yourself."

Allison knew she should tell Rho that Kim might be leaving for Hawaii with Jake—should she mention the allegations of drug dealing Kim obviously wasn't telling her about? How could she keep her best friend in ignorance?

"I need to know things as much as you do," Rhoda insisted, in the voice of a child. "Don't you know by now that Jake's a terrific guy?" Tears filled Rhoda's eyes. "Hang onto him, Allie, he's worth it—so is my Kim."

Allison studied her friend for a moment. "All right.

I'll fill you in," she said, leaning back. "But you can't mention any of this to anyone. Lives may depend on it."

Rhoda stared. "Lives?" Snatching a fresh tissue, she gulped, "I promise."

Allison spent the next half hour detailing Ross's plan to cover up his theft and disappear—with her.

"You should have told me sooner!" Rhoda exploded. "Don't you dare leave me out of this. I can help." Rhoda headed for the door, ready to do battle. "I'm going to find Kim and tell him you're crazy enough to let Ross take you out of the country. He and Jake will stop you."

"Kim already knows," Allison replied wearily. "I only told you because you promised to say nothing. I expect you to keep that promise."

Hands on hips, Rhoda took a no-nonsense pose. "Don't do this to Jake."

"Don't you see?" Allison sighed. "I love Jake too much to let him risk his future for me. This way is better."

"Wrong! Four heads are better than one halfwit," Rhoda huffed, "and that's exactly what you're acting like, Allison McKay. You've got two good friends and a man who loves you. Isn't that enough to handle that slimy Curran?"

"I told you, Ross has files that he can use to prove I'm guilty of defrauding the company of millions. And I can't disprove it. Boz knows I'm not guilty—but his word won't be enough to clear me."

"We'll just see about that," Rhoda declared. She drew her short frame up to military stiffness. "Kim and I will be at your place at eight o'clock tonight. Jake said you were expecting him, too." At the door,

Rhoda looked back. "We'll nail that Curran varmint one way or another. Count on it!"

Allison smiled in surrender. When Rhoda got her boilers stoked, she was hard to stop.

Shortly after eight, Jake received a call from Captain Heslip, confirming that Curran would be away from his apartment for the evening. Unofficially, if anyone took a look around, and left things undisturbed. . . . well, Heslip didn't need to know and wasn't going to ask.

Kim borrowed Rhoda's Taurus to make the night raid on Curran's apartment. Dull, dented and nondescript, it was perfect for the operation.

Dressed entirely in black to blend with the darkness, Jake and Kim crept over the security fence surrounding Curran's apartment. There was no moon to highlight their approach. Not a leaf stirred in the surrounding shrubbery. The heat inside their outfits was suffocating. In the stillness, every small sound was magnified.

Faint sounds drifting from the freeway blended with the tinny sounds of distant music emanating from the apartment's pool area. Jake knew they would be arrested for breaking and entering if they were caught, and Heslip wouldn't be able to help them.

They prepared to ascend. Jake tossed a padded scaling hook over the balcony of Curran's fourth floor apartment. Using the rappeling line he would later use to descend, he scaled the wall, with Kim climbing nimbly behind him.

Like shadows, they landed outside the targeted balcony door. A small night light burned inside.

Suddenly a dark shadow traversed the window, trailing past the six-inch opening in the balcony door. Jake raised his hand, signaling Kim to look. Then an angry meow emanated from behind the door, and Jake relaxed a little.

Curran's enormous Persian cat—a female, judging by the large pink silk bow around her neck—crouched low in the center of the room they were about to enter, hissing.

Kim worked his way cautiously behind the cat while Jake feinted toward her. Just as the cat was about to leap at Jake, in a blur of speed, Kim grabbed her by her thick scruff and emptied a pillowcase to contain her. Depositing the furious animal inside the improvised restraint, Kim knotted the end, making sure she could breathe but not get out.

"Decades of martial arts training and it takes two of us to catch a cat," Kim whispered.

Jake tried not to laugh. The situation was faintly absurd, but it was nonetheless dangerous. No one knew when Ross would return tonight.

The Persian scratched and squirmed to free herself, yowling plaintively. Speed was essential before the creature's frantic cries roused the suspicions of whoever might be in the next apartment.

"I wasn't expecting a killer kittycat," Jake whispered back. "There must be easier ways to make a living."

Kim shrugged. "We could make martial arts movies. But isn't this more fun?"

Jake nodded, and then snapped on a small high-intensity flashlight and sent its beam around the room.

A magnificent fruitwood bed stood against one wall and across from it was a small burled veneer Chinese desk. A highboy of matching wood stood against the third wall. Curran seemed quite good at spending other people's money. Jake's lips twitched in a grin. The bastard would have to leave everything behind when he split.

"You take the desk and I'll take the dresser," he whispered.

Silently the two men searched the apartment, taking care to put things back exactly as they'd found them.

After a few minutes, Jake straightened in triumph and motioned to Kim. He held an airline ticket from Guatemala City to Berne, Switzerland, that had been hidden beneath a stack of broadcloth shirts. The ticket, bearing the name Roger Carter, indicated one passenger and a cargo carrier. Apparently Curran didn't intend to take Allison with him any farther than Central America. A sudden vision of Curran killing Allison and burying her in a shallow grave in some remote jungle stabbed into Jake. He cursed silently. He would never allow Allison to leave Houston with that man.

After another fast sweep of the premises, Kim looked up, waving a schedule from a small airport just outside of Houston and a receipt from a private charter company for a prepaid flight to Guatemala City. The number of passengers listed was three. Curran, Allison and . . . did Curran have a hidden accomplice?

Jake's stomach knotted. The charter flight was scheduled to leave on Saturday. The day after tomorrow.

At the sound of an elevator stopping on the fourth floor, both men froze. Footsteps approached the apartment.

Kim raced for the cat and freed it from the pillowcase, while Jake took a final look around. Keeping his grip on the fierce feline's scruff, Kim gestured for Jake to get through the opening in the door. He followed, leaving one hand holding the cat inside the apartment. When he drew back, the cat ran in, meowing furiously—and Ross entered the apartment.

"What's the matter with Her Majesty tonight?" Ross said, crossing to lift the huge Persian into his arms. "It's only me. Relax. Did that nasty squirrel invade your balcony again?" Ross crooned softly to the cat as he placed her in the center of the bed and headed for the bathroom. Passing the balcony door, he closed it all the way and threw the bolt.

On the balcony, Jake and Kim waited silently. As soon as they heard water running in the shower, they rappeled swiftly down. Snapping the lines free from the balcony rail, they raced for the car. Now they knew when and where Curran planned to make his final move.

Jake and Kim hadn't returned to Allison's apartment, and the ice cream carton was close to empty. Tears made tiny star splashes on Rhoda's silk-clad bosom.

"Don't cry, Rho. Kim will be back soon. They know

what they're doing." If only Allison could believe that herself. She tried to take the ice cream carton from Rhoda, but her friend clung to it like a drowning man clinging to a life preserver.

"I didn't tell you everything. I found something among Kim's things at the dojang," Rho sobbed. "He and Jake are leaving Saturday for Honolulu!"

"So soon?"

"You already knew!" Rhoda squealed indignantly.

"Jake sort of mentioned it." Allison watched Rhoda gouge chunks of caramel praline ice cream from the Blue Bell container, sniffing between spoonfuls. "But how did you find out?" Allison skimmed a small bite of ice cream from the carton for herself, waiting for Rhoda to calm down and answer.

"I shouldn't have, but while I was waiting for Jake and Kim to finish class so I could bring them over here, I sort of snooped around Kim's quarters. There was this note . . . Kim obviously intended me to find *after* they were gone."

Shock stole Allison's breath away. Jake had lied to her. He'd said he might have to leave, but he had planned to be gone before she found out. Her lips twisted in an ironic smile. What a joke! All that business about duty to his *sensei,* a life debt to Kim, had to be part of an even bigger lie to escape any long-term commitment on his part. How he must have laughed inwardly when she told him she loved him.

"I only knew Jake might be leaving to take care of some business in Honolulu," Allison admitted, choked with emotion, "but I didn't realize it might be so soon—like this Saturday." Jake hadn't said lots of things. Maybe the silent Jake was the real Jake.

Maybe he'd never meant to let her into his life, and this secret departure was all part of his easy letdown.

"What else did the note say?" Allison felt compelled to ask.

Rhoda spooned a huge bite of ice cream into her mouth, and shivered all over.

She paused, waiting for her tongue to thaw. "The note was to both of us. It said Kim and Jake were called to Honolulu." Rhoda scrubbed her eyes with the heels of her hands. "We were supposed to find the note when we came to class on Saturday—Kim was going to up and leave, damn him!" Rhoda sobbed pitifully.

"So they planned to slip away without us knowing," Allison mused. "It doesn't make sense. Jake and Kim wouldn't leave the dojang just when it's starting to succeed. There's something else behind this."

"That's just it," Rhoda sobbed, more in control now. "The note said they had to return to Honolulu to clear up some drug dealing charge made against them. Did you know about this?" Rho raised an accusing brow.

Allison nodded and took her hand.

"Let me explain—"

"And that isn't all," Rhoda barreled on. "After I found the note, I looked through Kim's things and found an envelope from Graham Insurance. It was a notice addressed to Jake Tory and Kim Joon, advising them that their loan had been called due. That's more likely why they're leaving." Rhoda snuffled and blew her nose. "It said they had to pay the entire amount in full immediately or forfeit the money they'd already paid down."

Jake hadn't mentioned that he'd known about the loan call.

Rhoda ignored the melting ice cream leaking down the sides of the container. "So I guess Jake and Kim are out of business. There's no need now for them to ever come back from Hawaii."

"Boz didn't call that loan," Allison said. "Somehow Ross got the notice through the system." She handed Rhoda a fistful of tissues and gestured toward her nose. "Jake did say that Boz would never permit Curran to get away with that. They aren't leaving on that account. This is Ross Curran's doing."

Rhoda shoved Allison's spoon back into her hand.

Allison took a bite of ice cream, allowing its satiny coolness to slip down her throat.

Ross had agreed not to act on the loan call or the drug charges if she went with him without a struggle. But he hadn't waited. That meant he was about to take off, whether she agreed to go quietly or not.

"Could Ross have actually written the notice himself?" Rhoda asked, licking the back of her spoon. Wadding up a tissue, she threw it in the wastebasket as if she were body-slamming Ross. "He's just mean enough to do something like that."

Allison tossed her spoon in the now empty ice cream container, keeping her blackest thoughts to herself. *Ross Curran would leave nothing but a wasteland behind.* Would that wasteland include dead bodies?

The walls seemed to enclose Allison in a suffocating embrace. Dimly she heard Rhoda's sobs, but she couldn't respond. *Jake wouldn't simply tuck tail and run—but all the evidence pointed that way.*

Within five minutes, Allison's life lay shattered.

Ross intended ruining four lives, and he was about to get away with it.

She glanced at her watch, staring anxiously at Rho. "Where can Jake be? Could Ross have caught them in his apartment? Shot them for burglars?" Allison turned on the TV. Maybe a late-breaking report would tell them if anyone had been caught breaking and entering—and had been shot.

Allison turned to Rhoda. "Did you see the loan notice itself, or just a letter referring to it?" That was one area she felt competent to deal with. "I want to see that loan notice for myself. I want Jake to look me in the eye and tell me he meant to leave without saying a word, leave a debt unpaid. He may go, but not until he faces me." Allison's stone-hard gaze reflected her sense of betrayal.

She snatched up the phone.

At the dojang, Jake ignored the ringing phone, but Kim raced to answer anyway.

Their stealthy visit to Ross's apartment had been a success, and Jake was packing the last of their equipment for shipment. If the loan call was authentic, they'd have to abandon the dojang to their creditors.

They had peeled off their black clothing to return to Allison's apartment. As soon as they were far away from Curran's apartment, Jake had phoned Captain Heslip at HPD and given him the information about the airline tickets.

Jake had just crammed the last of his gear in a duffel when Kim returned from the phone.

"That was Uncle calling from Honolulu," Kim

shouted jubilantly. "*Sensei* said the Houston Police phoned him and explained that the drug charges were false. We don't have to go to Hawaii."

Jake's hands stilled on the duffel.

"But we're not out of the woods yet. Don't forget that our loan from Graham is now due and payable. In full," he said, yanking on a strap.

Kim unfolded his lithe form from the pillow where he'd finally relaxed.

"Mr. Graham didn't authorize it," Kim insisted, pacing around the tatami mat. "The notice was signed by 'Officer in Charge,' and the signature was blurred." He re-read the notice and lifted a questioning brow. "Curran?"

Jake nodded, reaching for the plum wine he'd left until last. He poured a small cup for each of them, then raised his own.

"Here's to us, old friend. There's only one more hill to climb—and we'll climb it together."

"Right!" Kim shouted exultantly, downing his wine.

Jake grinned. Rhoda had been good for Kim.

Across the dojang, the office phone rang once, then went silent. He shrugged. Whoever called must have been too impatient to wait.

Jake smiled. Their silent visit to Curran had taken more time than anticipated. Even so, he needed to see Allison, tell her he wouldn't be leaving—ever.

Kim fell into step with Jake.

"I plan to have a word with Rho. I think she's been snooping through my things."

Jake grinned. "She's your problem, brother."

"Yeah, but what a wonderful problem!" Kim exclaimed.

"Where did you put the loan notice?" Jake asked, suddenly.

Kim slapped his forehead, then grinned sheepishly.

"She knows!" they said together.

Thirteen

Allison slammed down the phone, anger overriding her fear for Jake. "I'm not waiting any longer! I'm going over to the dojang. Stay here, Rho, and keep calling them."

"What if they show up after you leave?"

"Keep them here. Don't say anything about what you know. Wait until I get back. If they aren't there, then they may have left for Hawaii already."

Allison grabbed her purse and car keys and raced through the door. The idea of Jake's sneaking off sent Allison's temper soaring. The wine was chilled, a late supper was ready for the four of them, and Jake and Kim hadn't even had the decency to call. They were supposed to make plans tonight for trapping Ross. "I'll murder the rat—and without using karate," she growled.

Blinded by angry tears, Allison burned rubber climbing the parking ramp to head for the dojang.

Jake whirled at the sound of skidding tires just as Allison's Celica crunched to a halt outside the dojang.

"We were on our way—"

"Yeah. Sure. On your way out of town!" Allison wrenched open the door, leaving the car parked at a precarious angle, its engine still racing from the breakneck drive over. Her heartache had hardened into rage.

Jake's eyes widened. "What's this all about, Allison? I told you we'd be there as soon as we left Ross's and got cleaned up. Why are you so angry?" Jake's innocent expression cranked Allison's temper up another notch.

"You lied to me! How could I have been stupid enough to believe you loved me and wanted to protect me? One way or another, all you men are alike." Words tumbled out on a river of brimstone, making no sense, but she couldn't stop them. She raised a fist, but Jake fended off the blow easily and hustled her to the idling car. Shoving her inside, he reached to fasten her seat belt.

"Haven't you learned better than that yet?" He grinned, enjoying her outrage. "Cool off until we get to your place and unravel this mystery."

Kim vaulted into Rho's Taurus and followed as Jake gunned away from the curb.

"We're going to settle this lunacy, starting with why you're trying to knock my head off."

Allison rode in stony silence, her arms clamped across her chest, her eyes fixed straight ahead. If he thought he could bounce into her life and out again at his pleasure, he could think again.

Jake negotiated the distance to the condo and raced the car down the ramp amid a shower of sparks when the tailpipe struck concrete. Dragging up the parking brake, he brought the car to a bone-jarring halt.

"Upstairs!" he ordered, through clenched teeth, his own anger blossoming. Pulling Allison none too gently from the car, he nudged her ahead of him. Kim moved double time to keep up with Jake's angry strides.

Rhoda met them at the door, a ring of ice cream on her upper lip. "You're still here!" She threw her arms around Kim, transferring her ice cream mustache to him.

Kim licked his upper lip and smiled down at the grinning blonde in his arms. "Looks like it," he teased, feeling his arms and checking his face. "We weren't leaving until Saturday—but then you know that, don't you?" he said, lifting a teasing brow. Rhoda blushed a deep rose. Grasping his hand, she dragged him into Allison's bedroom and shut the door. For a while, soft murmurs emanated from the room, then there was silence.

Jake drew Allison down onto the sofa beside him. "Let's get the anger out of the way first, then perhaps you'd like to explain what set you off."

"I don't owe you an explanation. If there's any explaining to do, you're the one who needs to do it," Allison said icily. That damned discipline of Jake's usually kept his fires banked. She wanted to see him blow his top, lose his cool—and she wanted him to kiss her, long and hot.

Jake stared, trying to read the fleeting emotions sliding across Allison's face.

"What is it you want from me? I love you. Isn't that enough to earn your trust? Where did you think I was going, except back to you?"

"When you said you were honor bound to return to Hawaii, you failed to mention it would be Saturday—and without notice to anyone. I never thought you would just slip away without saying a word—after saying you loved me—wanted to protect me." Her eyes blazed and her red hair seemed to crackle as she added another stone to the heap of grievances.

"And what makes you think you can shove me around the way you did just now?" She rubbed her aching arm where Jake had hustled her into the apartment. "I'll never learn!" she cried, her lip curling in self-disgust.

Jake's steely discipline was firmly back in place.

"Every word I said to you was true." He nudged her head up. "I *do* love you, and Kim and I weren't leaving until Curran was caught. We found enough information in his apartment tonight to head him off before he goes a mile. I called in the information to Captain Heslip at the Houston Police Department, and he's taking over." Jake pulled Allison hard against him. "You need to learn that things operate differently in my world, Allison. When I thought I might be forced to leave, it seemed better for me to go without telling you. If I never came back, then I'd let you hate me as it seems you do."

Allison caught their reflection in the mirror. She couldn't hate Jake. They belonged in each other's arms.

Jake took Allison's hand and raised it to his lips.

"Before you came barreling up to the dojang, Kim received a phone call from our *sensei* in Honolulu. He said the Houston police made it clear that the allegations of drug dealing were phony. Heslip explained that someone was trying to set us up."

"But Rhoda told me—"

Jake lifted his arms in despair. "Kim can't keep a

thing from Rhoda. It's a good thing he doesn't know any nuclear secrets."

Allison decided not to mention Rho's prying into Kim's papers.

Jake glanced toward the closed bedroom door and settled Allison's suddenly unresisting body more comfortably against his shoulder. "Even though the police officially confirmed that the drug charges are false, Kim and I still may have had to go to our *sensei* to explain things. I warned you that karate masters are often not their own men."

Then Allison burst out without thinking. "That rat Ross didn't wait! He promised not to call your loan if I—well, I should have known a promise from Ross isn't worth the gunpowder to blow it to hell. Why didn't you tell me that you already knew about it?"

Jake's hands fell to his sides. "I can straighten out the matter of the loan with Graham, but how could you ever suppose I'd let you go with Curran just to save my hide?" A dangerous glint entered Jake's eyes. He'd be there ahead of him when Curran headed for the airport Saturday.

"Promise you won't go near Ross," Allison pleaded. "He's far more dangerous than I ever dreamed—and now he's desperate."

Jake stared past Allison's shoulder without replying.

Allison studied Jake's taut features. What had happened to the quiet, serene man she'd first seen in the shadows of the recreation room—the man so silent, so gathered within himself? Had she stripped him of his discipline? Briefly, he'd been murderously angry, and all because of her.

"Curran plans to leave day after tomorrow." Jake

caressed her cheek idly, as though his mind was elsewhere.

"Then let the police handle him," Allison said.

"But what if the police fail to catch him? He's clever. And what about my promise to Boz?"

"Jake, are you absolutely certain Ross leaves Saturday?"

Jake gave her an enigmatic smile. "Trust me. I'm sure." He stood. "Now, get Kim and Rho in here and we'll talk."

The four gathered around the dinette table with their coffee. Allison's carefully prepared dinner was dried out, but no one seemed to mind. The candles had burned down, and the wine was back in the fridge.

"My office is next to old Cream of the Crap Curran," Rho said. She had that belligerent look again. "I can watch him during work hours, and tell Kim if he alters his usual routine." She rubbed her hands together gleefully. "I know just how to annoy him. I'll drop in on him a dozen times a day with weather reports and meaningless chatter." Anticipation turned Rho's cheeks a lively pink.

"You do that, Little Bird." Kim squeezed Rho's hand. "Jake and I will divide our time watching Curran's apartment. If he makes any detours, one of us will know. Sooner or later, he'll try to get to any money he hasn't already sent out of the country."

Allison felt a frisson of fear that sent shivers up her spine. If Ross eluded the trap . . . she had no idea what would happen to her.

"I'll meet with Boz and find out how the loan call got through the system without being detected. Then, I'll see that it's canceled." She had a more important job than that to do, but Jake mustn't know she planned to go to see Ross.

Jake scraped his chair back and stood.

"Don't go to Graham just yet. Curran has assumed that Graham thinks you're the guilty party. Let him keep thinking that. Let him believe his set-up is fool-proof—that his attempts to frame me and Kim on drug charges and scare us with that loan call are all still in operation." Jake paced from the kitchen to the table several times, before he said, "Captain Heslip told me that the Drug Agency monitors all calls as soon as a snitch contacts them. If Curran should phone his charter plane, Heslip will know."

"But what about Honolulu?" Rhoda turned anxious brown eyes on Jake.

"We're not going. Kim must have been too . . . engrossed to tell you." Jake sent a wicked grin Kim's way.

"We only heard that we didn't have to go tonight," Kim grumbled, examining his toes, avoiding Rho's eyes. "I spoke to my uncle and he said it wouldn't be necessary."

"Some Koreans move fast, except for our Kim here," Jake said, dropping a hand on Kim's shoulder. "Anyway, right now, dealing with Curran is priority one."

Jake moved up behind Allison's chair, and began a slow massage on the rigid muscles of her neck. "Relax. I'll explain in detail later," he whispered.

She nodded. But after he left, she was going to call Boswell Graham and do what she had to do.

* * *

Much later, when the men had left, Allison rang Boz's number. He answered immediately.

"I'm sorry to call at this hour, Boz," Allison began, "but I need to see you in the morning, and no one must know."

"By no one, you mean Curran?" Boz asked, dryly. "Who else mustn't know? Tory?" Boz cleared his throat. "Talk, Allison."

Allison gripped the phone tightly. "We can't discuss any of this over the phone, but I have an update on matters that concern us both."

"If there were any other way, Allison, I wouldn't involve you, but you're just the hook I need to land a certain fish." Boz's voice dropped. Allison heard a match scratch and pictured her boss lighting his one-a-day cigar. "I knew he'd find a way to involve you sooner or later because of the job you hold with the company. Curran had to involve the claims clearance person—in other words, you. He didn't count on my knowing you so well," Boz chuckled rustily.

His gratified sigh seemed to echo in her ear. Boz was no doubt happily wreathed in a cloud of cigar smoke.

"If you don't want the job, Allison, I'll understand."

"Yes, but you might never recover what you've already—"

Boz had just offered her an out—a way to keep Jake from doing something desperate. "Thanks, but I'm still interested in the job. I'm not afraid." That had to be the biggest lie she'd ever told. She wasn't just afraid—she was *terrified.*

"I thought you'd say that, Allison. You've got grit to go with that red hair. I expect total success from our next vice president." Boz chuckled at Allison's gasp of surprise. "You may as well know now. You'll find out at the next board meeting anyway."

Boz's gruff, fatherly voice brought tears to Allison's eyes. Everything she'd worked for was within reach. For a moment, she couldn't speak. Why had Boz told her about her promotion now? Everything hung in the balance: Jake, her life, their future together. She might never claim any of it, if Ross had his way.

"I'll do my best, you know that."

"That I do, Allison. Seven tomorrow morning? Usual place. Leave your car down the block by the bank building and walk."

"I'll be there." Allison paused. "Thanks for everything, Boz," she whispered, cradling the phone.

Fourteen

The proof of Ross's getaway plans was in the hands of the police, but Jake couldn't shake his icy fear for Allison.

Kim sensed Jake's tension. He dropped his arm across Jake's shoulders.

"Don't worry, brother, we'll be at the airport before that plane leaves Houston."

Jake pounded his fist in his palm, his dark eyes flashing fire. "We can't slip up." His gaze lingered a moment on his friend. "You don't have to be there. I can handle this alone. Stay with Rhoda and wait for me."

"I'll be there!" Kim bit out the words, his dark brows lifted indignantly.

Jake grasped Kim's wrists.

"I already owe you my life. Don't double the debt."

"Where do you want me positioned?" Kim asked, ignoring Jake's objections.

"Right at my side . . . brother."

Allison dragged herself out of bed, and staggered to the kitchen. She looked into the coffee pot, hoping for a few drops of last night's coffee, and found her hopes fulfilled.

"Sludge," she sighed.

She scowled at the inky substance she'd poured into her cup, then shoved it into the microwave. "Anything to jumpstart my heart," she muttered, dragging her hands through her tangled mop of red hair. She dropped into a chair, trying to keep her eyes open until the microwave dinged.

She had to dress and leave for the office, and Jake still hadn't called.

"Got any of that left?" Rhoda, who'd slept over, stuck her tousled head through the kitchen door and nodded toward the coffeepot. She'd slept in her slip and now wore Allison's ratty chenille bathrobe. It looked every bit as unflattering on Rho as it did on her, Allison thought, and made a mental note to give it back to the Salvation Army store where she'd gotten it in the first place.

"If you're into dregs, there's plenty." Allison waved a limp hand toward the coffee pot.

Rho risked a sip and wrinkled her nose.

"This is beyond awful. But thanks anyway."

Rhoda took both cups to the sink, muttering about used coffee and some people's hospitality.

"I'm going home to change. Then I'll head to the office to keep an eye on Ross Curran. I'll let you know if he so much as moves a muscle."

Allison gave her a thumbs-up, and checked the clock on the microwave. A little over an hour remained before she had to meet Boz.

Allison had left Boz's office, reassured that Jake's loan for the dojang would not be called in. Now, she was slumped behind her desk, her mind a sea of misery. Why did she have to fall in love with Jake? But time for regrets was past. She would love Jake for the rest of her life—however long or short that might be.

Ross glanced up sharply when Allison shoved open the door to his office. An artificial smile spread on his face, but his unblinking stare let her know she wasn't exactly welcome.

"What can I do for you, Allie dear?" He glanced uneasily at the papers on his desk, quickly turning them facedown.

Allison fought back her disgust and met his stare. "I have a proposition for you." She sidled around him, but he blocked her view of the exposed papers. Allison sat. "Two million," she said bluntly.

"What do you mean?" Ross moved closer and perched on the edge of his desk between Allison and the papers he was trying to hide.

"I want two million of the money you stole from Graham, and I'll front for you until you can get out of the country. If you don't, I'll confess and name you as my accomplice. By the time you lie your way out of it, you'll be on every front page in the state. What's it worth to keep me quiet—and keep the heat off you?"

Ross sent her a look of grudging admiration.

"I didn't think you had it in you, Allie. But your demands are quite out of the question. I don't have to give you anything. I'll be gone before you can—" He clamped his jaw and glared at her.

Allison grinned. "Try again, Ross." The air conditioner came on, ruffling the papers on Ross's desk. He slapped a hand behind him to anchor them.

"Now, Allie. Let's not be nasty. What if I agreed to give you, say, two hundred thousand? Surely you could go a long way on that."

"Cut the crap, Ross! I've got you and you know it. Besides, think of all the things we could do—if we went away together."

Ross turned a venomous look on her.

"You may not know it, Allie, but you never had a choice about going with me—and you can forget about the money."

Allison leaned over and picked up Ross's Mont Blanc pen, but she still couldn't see the papers he was hiding.

Allison took a deep breath. "We don't have to stay together, once we get away . . . unless you want to." She leaned back in her chair and waggled the pen between her fingers. "Now that you have all those millions, we could live a life of luxury." Allison wanted to scream. Damn Ross's poker face. "Let's not be enemies," she coaxed. "Isn't it better to be friends? There's a whole world waiting for us—all it takes is money."

Her gaze moved over Ross's bruised face. It had begun to heal, but the scar on his lip would never disappear.

"I'm sorry Jake hurt you, but I see there's no real damage. You're as handsome as ever." Allison caught her breath. How much of this malarkey could she spout before she threw up? How much of it would Ross believe?

Ross remained stock still, allowing his gaze to travel the length of Allison's crossed legs.

"Really, my dear? I had no idea how much you admired me. Until now, you've given every indication of hating my guts. When you fought me so vigorously in your apartment, all I saw was loathing in your eyes. Was that just show, or was it a turn-on for you?" Ross circled the desk and came to stand by Allison's chair.

"Could be," Allison said in her sultriest tone. "I've known stranger things to happen."

"I thought you were in love with the karate man. Why do you want to go with me and leave him—aside from the money, of course?"

"Jake tried his luck with me for a while, but it didn't take. Ask Rhoda. I'm too smart to go for a martial arts master who lives on rice and tofu when I can have millions with you." *Forgive me, Jake.*

"Fat chance I'd ask that fat little Rhoda anything," Ross spat. "She's started clinging to me like stink on a skunk." He laughed nastily. "Maybe your plump little friend is in love with me, too."

Allison flinched at the thought of what Rhoda would say—and do—if she'd heard Ross say that. Drawing a deep breath, she went on.

"You were really quite clever, Ross—figuring a way to get your hands on all that money without being caught."

Ross stroked a hand down his designer-logo tie. "I was rather clever, wasn't I?" He sneaked a look at his papers to make sure they were still well hidden. "I'll give some thought to what you suggest. It might be simpler to get away without making waves, if we stay together." His eyes raked Allison. "It might not be too bad having a beautiful redhead on my arm when I reach . . . Either way, I think I'll take you along, as a companion—or as a hostage."

How much of what he was saying was reliable? Boz had said he didn't believe Ross would leave an uncollected million behind. Could the crazy creep reach it before Saturday? A wild hope flared in Allison's chest, then quickly dashed. Even if the police caught him, the remaining millions were still missing.

"I'd be crazy to miss out on an opportunity to see Europe on millions." Allison tried what she hoped was a convincing simper. "We can live like royalty—have new names. We might even—"

"I'll decide what we might do," Ross cut in. He stood abruptly. "Go back to your office. You shouldn't be seen here. I'll have to make a few arrangements first—if I take you *all* the way." Circling his desk, Ross swept the papers he'd been guarding into a drawer.

"The charter plane from Houston is no problem," he muttered, thinking aloud, "but I'll need another ticket from Guatemala City to—" He looked at Allison and grinned. "Wouldn't you like to know where?"

Allison kept her expression bland, but a clammy chill warned her that Ross was really deciding whether she would live or die—whether he'd let her get past Central America—or whether she'd get on the plane at all.

"I have to pack and get ready," Allison said. "When will we leave?" Better to behave as though she'd be going with him—that she had nothing to fear—and that she knew nothing about Saturday.

"Don't bother to pack. We'll buy what we need on the way. After all, there'll be plenty of money once we get there."

Allison sent him a brilliant smile. "I hope 'there'

is Paris. I've always wanted to own a couturier gown." She waited, but her little bit of bait wasn't taken.

"You'll just love where you're going," Ross said nastily. "Leave that to me."

Allison forced an eager smile. "Than we *are* going together?"

Ross wouldn't answer. He checked his intercom to make sure it was switched off, then locked the door.

Allison's heart took an erratic leap. Surely Ross wouldn't try anything right here in the office.

"I'll leave everything to you," Allison said shakily. Rising, she slipped into a subtle defensive position, in case he came at her. He'd never touch her again, even if it ruined the show. But when he showed no signs of reaching for her, she edged toward the door and flipped the lock open. When he didn't try to stop her, she slipped into the hall. Whatever reason Ross had locked the door, it hadn't been to keep her in, but to keep someone else out.

Out in the hall, Allison heard the lock click behind her. She could hear Ross whistling the way he did when he'd brought off a successful deal.

By five o'clock, Jake still hadn't contacted her. Where the hell was he? She refused to think of all the things that could have happened, or she'd go nuts.

There was no answer at 3B, nor at the dojang when Allison phoned again. Rhoda had left the office at five, after promising to let her know if Kim called.

A quiver of uneasiness wormed its way into Allison's brain. Something wasn't right here.

* * *

Jake was stretched out on the sofa when Allison opened the door to 3A.

"Jake! Why didn't you call? I've been so—" She stopped herself. He didn't have to report to her.

"There were things I had to do." He swung his legs over the side of the sofa and came to her. "I'm staying here tonight. Curran's not the kind to pass up taking revenge on me—and hurting you is the only way he can."

"God, Jake, what have I done to you?"

Jake's grim expression frightened Allison. His words were those of a lover, not those of a cool, controlled bodyguard.

"Come." He lifted her in his arms and carried her to the bed and laid her down and propped himself against the headboard beside her. "I wasn't hired to do this." He kissed her gently, allowing his lips to rove her cheeks and eyelids and come to rest against her ear. "I started out to guard a beautiful redhead at her employer's request, but everything has changed. I love you, Allison. Believe that."

She nearly wept.

I had you, and you were all I wanted or needed. Soon, I might not even have you, she thought, still determined not to tell him about her plan to outfox Curran. There would be no way to keep Jake safe if she did.

Jake studied Allison's face. He reached out to gently stroke her hair, savoring the silky feel of it, inhaling her fragrance. Breathing quietly, Jake closed his eyes and held her close until she did the same.

Allison stirred. Drowsy words escaped her lips, "I love you, Jake." He tightened his hold on her.

"I love you, too, Allison."

Fifteen

Even before she opened her eyes Allison knew Jake was gone.

Stumbling into the living room, her eyes fell on a scrap of paper lying on the sofa.

> Went next door to change.
> Back soon. Don't leave without me.
> I love you. Jake.

How long had he been gone? Panic gripped her. She hadn't heard him leave, but then Jake moved with the silence of smoke.

She still wore the sweats she'd worn the night before when Jake had put her to bed. She looked in the mirror. Her hair was a disaster. Spiky red locks framed her face like a clown's wig. If she hurried, she could shower before Jake returned.

She'd just turned on the tap when a knock came. *Jake!* She flew to the door and flung it open, a glad smile on her face.

"Good morning, Allie." Shouldering his way through the door, Ross kicked it shut behind him, He carried a large leather briefcase under one arm.

He eyed Allison's rumpled sweats and tousled hair with evident distaste.

"What are you doing here, Ross?" She tried to appear cool, but inside her guts churned like a drive-through car wash.

"Don't make a fuss. We're leaving now. Just keep your mind on all those couturier gowns you'll be buying." Ross took Allison's elbow and dragged her toward the door.

"But you were supposed to let me know!" Allison dug her heels in, her heart pounding wildly. She slipped into her role of willing accomplice. "No need to be so rough! Give me a minute to shower and change. You should have warned me we were leaving today." Her eyes slid toward 3B, praying that Jake would somehow know that Ross was here—and leaving ahead of schedule.

"Don't take me for a fool, Allison. You're stalling for time to alert Graham, and your karate man. Now why would I allow you to do that?" Ross clutched his briefcase, and dragged open the door with his other arm.

"Don't be stupid, Ross. There's no need to force me. I told you I wanted to go with you. Why should I call Boz when we'd both be arrested? At least let me dress! I can't travel in sweats." She scrubbed her damp palms down her pants legs, sending a frantic glance in the direction of Jake's apartment.

"I'll need at least a few clothes for the trip! Sweats would only call attention to us." Ross was a pretentious snob who wouldn't want to be seen with her dressed like this—unless he didn't intend for her ever to be seen again.

Allison craned her head toward the bedroom, glancing frantically at the balcony doors. Help was only a few feet away, but the doors were bolted.

"Quit stalling, Allie. We're leaving." Ross propped open the door with his foot.

Fear congealed in Allison's stomach. Now that the moment of truth had come, she was paralyzed.

But Ross gave her no time for regret. He dragged her through the door, his fingers biting painfully into her arms.

"Why are you doing this?" Allison panted, trying to keep pace with Ross. "There's still at least a million left to be collected."

"Let's start off right," Ross growled. "You don't ask—I don't answer."

Boz had gambled on Ross's greed, on his wanting to collect the money on those last few fire claims before he made his move. But Boz had been wrong—they'd all been wrong. Ross had the cunning of a fox—and absolutely no conscience.

Allison ground her teeth in frustration. There was no sound from 3B. When Jake returned and found her gone, he'd have no idea where she was. How could she let him know she hadn't gone of her own free will?

"Move it!" Ross pushed Allison toward the elevator. With his elbow, he pressed the down button, keeping a firm grip on Allison and the briefcase.

Allison tasted raw fear. Jake's door remained closed. *Please, God, let him walk out of his door and see us before it's too late.* But in the next breath, she prayed he wouldn't see them. Ross was desperate enough to kill Jake. She felt like a captured bird staring at a cobra. There would be no way to trace their movements.

When the elevator reached garage level, Ross shoved Allison out. His BMW was parked in the basement near Allison's Celica.

"Over here. Shake it up! Dragging your feet won't bring your boyfriend to our little get-together. You know"—Ross yanked open the door to his car—"you're lucky I changed my mind. I was going to leave you dead. That's why I was following you. If that old lady hadn't pulled you back from falling under the bus, I wouldn't have had to change my plans at all." He chuckled softly. "Now I can never let you get away."

Fear made Allison's stomach clench. Desperate, she slipped off the green and gold paisley scarf belting her sweats and dropped it beside her Celica. Jake would recognize it immediately. The scarf had become a joke between them ever since he'd suggested she find another belt to wear with her *gi*. When he found her gone and saw the scarf beside her car, would he recognize it as a signal that Ross had moved early? It was all she could do. It wasn't as if Ross was going to let her leave a note on the windshield.

A deadly calm descended on Allison. She had no one but herself to count on now.

Ross shoved her roughly into the seat of his car and turned the key in the ignition. The low throb of the powerful engine reverberated through the confined underground area, echoing the steady pounding of Allison's heart. It was obvious that Ross hadn't believed a single word of her story about wanting to share the loot and his life. Four million dollars was enough incentive for a man like him to clear away any obstacles from his path—beginning with Allison McKay.

Sixteen

"Allison? Open up, it's Jake." He pressed his ear against her door. He could hear the shower running. She would step out any minute and answer the door. But instinct told him to make sure. He turned back to 3B and crossed over the balconies, jimmied the door, and entered through the patio. The shower was on in the bathroom, but there was no sound or movement.

"Allison?" Jake's heart lurched. Maybe she'd fallen. He pushed open the door and looked around. Although the shower ran full blast, Allison was not there. An acid rush of dread flooded his stomach. She was gone—and she probably hadn't left on her own.

Jake took the stairs to the garage two at a time. Allison's car was still in its slot. Then he spotted her paisley scarf lying on the pavement. The maintenance man was just leaving his small office below the stairs and Jake called to him.

"Did you see anyone in the garage just now?"

"There was that fellow with the fancy foreign car. Miss McKay and him took off together."

"How long ago?" Jake kept his voice level.

"Five minutes, give or take," the man said, eyeing Jake curiously.

Jake ran Allison's scarf through his fingers. This could be her signal to him, if Ross had kicked off his plan ahead of schedule and had taken her with him. He fought to center his thoughts. He would need Kim's help, and he had to let Graham and the police know that Ross had left and taken Allison. They should be on their way to the airport this minute.

Jake located Allison's spare key under the Celica's fender and slid behind the wheel, burning rubber as he tore out of the garage on his way to the dojang. Rhoda and Kim were just coming out.

"Ross took Allison! Kim, call the police. Tell Captain Heslip to send back-up to Mims Airport, then meet me there."

"I'm on my way!" Kim waved Jake ahead and ran back into the dojang.

Rhoda jumped into her Taurus and revved the engine, ready to take off the minute Kim returned.

Jake skidded the Celica to a halt at the airport and leaped out.

A Lear jet sat on the runway ready for takeoff, but outside of dust blowing across the barren field, nothing stirred. The scene was almost two-dimensional in its static silence. Then the BMW drove up, headed for the entrance to the boarding area. Jake watched Ross and Allison get out, but he stayed out of sight.

Ross shoved Allison through the terminal door. "Get moving. The plane will take off the moment we board." He jabbed the barrel of his pistol into

Allison's ribs, silencing her. She could only pray Jake had found the scarf she had dropped.

"Stop thinking so hard, Allie, I'll do that for you." Ross's tone was sneering. He seemed to be already celebrating his victory. He raised his head to look around. Not a soul moved near the baggage and cargo areas. Even the traffic on the highway was muffled and remote. His eyes panned the perimeter of the airfield. There was nothing but a beat-up old car with a mechanic bent under its hood.

A stray dog trotted across the grass bordering the tarmac, pausing once or twice to sniff before lifting his leg against a tall weed.

"In less than an hour, we'll be over the Gulf and on our way to Guatemala," Ross muttered, dragging Allison behind him. She heard the pilot rev the jet's engines, rending the silence.

Nausea struck the back of Allison's throat. The doorway to freedom lay open to Ross, and there was no one to stop him—no one but her.

"Now, Allie!" Ross shouted. "Run for the plane." He took off, dragging her faster, the briefcase clutched under his arm. In his other hand he carried a large animal carrier.

A pounding began in Allison's head. He would either dispose of her as soon as they reached Central America . . . or now. She felt the hard thrust of a pistol in her side.

"We can't go far without passports," Allison gasped, tossing out objections as she trotted to keep up.

Ross barely spared Allison a glance. He had stopped off just long enough to grab Allison and collect Her Majesty from the cattery where he'd stashed her.

Shoulders hunched, the cat carrier banging against his leg, Ross sprinted for the plane's open door.

Before he reached the steps, Allison stopped in her tracks and wrenched her arm free. She bent over, her heart hammering in her chest.

Ross turned, snarling. "Move!" He scrabbled for his gun.

"I think I'm going to be sick." Allison retched convincingly, aiming directly at Ross's expensive shoes. He drew back in disgust.

"Puke in the plane." He nudged Allison ahead of him, pressing the gun against her spine.

At the bottom of the boarding steps, Allison managed another realistic retch, turning back as though she would hurl on his designer suit.

At the sound of running footsteps, Ross whirled to see police and plainclothesmen closing in from all sides with Jake in the lead. He swung the gun wildly, his eyes glazed with hatred.

Pointing the gun at Allison's temple, Ross shouted for the charter pilot to get ready for takeoff.

"All of you stop where you are, unless you want to see this woman's brains splattered all over the runway."

Bent over as she was, Allison was able to unfasten the latch on the cat's cage. Frightened by the plane's engines, the huge Persian sprang from her cage and raced across the tarmac. The stray dog took up the chase, barking gleefully after the cat. Ross's attention wavered toward Her Majesty, who was about to be overtaken by the dog.

Allison jumped away and, rising on one leg, she

quickly switched legs, firing her anchor leg, heel forward, to catch Ross squarely in the crotch. He doubled over, writhing in pain. The gun clattered to the ground.

After that, everything happened quickly. Ross groveled on the ground at Allison's feet, and a triumphant screech from across the tarmac told her that Her Majesty had also escaped her pursuer.

Jake skidded to a stop beside Allison and dragged her into his arms.

"Well done!" he laughed, trying to still his trembling. "You said you didn't need me, and you didn't!"

"But I did need you, Jake! I was so scared!" Words tumbled from Allison's lips. "I didn't know what I was doing. I just reacted blindly. With all the karate lessons you gave me, the only thing I could think of was the one you called the Crippled Crane defense." She laid her head on his shoulder. The sound of Jake's heart pounding beneath her ear was reassuring, but she shivered when she thought of what might have happened had her wild kick failed . . .

"Warrior lady," Jake whispered, a wide grin on his face, "you'll be a master of martial arts yet."

As if! "By the way, how did you know—?"

Jake simply handed her the scarf.

"I'll tell you later, love," he groaned, silencing her with a kiss. He decided to wait until she was calmer to tell her that he'd never seen a cleaner defense kick in all his years in martial arts. He'd been right about Allison—she was a piece of work—a brave, funny piece of work—and she was his.

"Should we call Boz?" she asked shakily.

"Let the police do that. You'll have to give them

a statement eventually, but right now they're busy here."

Ross Curran's cat had been rounded up, with only a minimal loss of fur and was on her way back to the cattery. The police were packing up. Through the squad car window, Ross's face was a mask of hatred, and Allison shivered again and looked away.

"Congratulations, Allison. You nabbed the bad guy," Jake said solemnly. Despite his grave expression, his shoulders shook with laughter. "I think I'll add your Crippled Crane move to my karate course. It's unorthodox, but it works!" Then his laughter burst forth, despite Jake's efforts. "Of course," he gasped, catching his breath, "you'll have to teach it to me first."

Allison looked into Jake's dark eyes, sparkling with mischief. "Was I that bad?"

"No, love, you were that *good.*"

Jake was about to drive away, when Kim raced to the side of the car.

"Where are you two going?"

Jake looked up and smiled. "Brother, thanks for your help. But I think Allison and I need to be alone now."

At the dojang, Jake went directly to his office, and returned to drop down onto a cushion beside Allison.

"This is for you, Warrior Woman," Jake said, handing Allison a yellow belt to wear with her *gi.* "After today, you've earned your first degree in tae kwon do. Not exactly in the way I planned it, but you earned it just the same. Maybe now you'll give up this thing." Jake reached in his pocket and handed Allison her paisley scarf, smiling wryly.

Allison took it from his hand. "That scarf saved my life. You wouldn't have known where I was if I hadn't left it for you to find."

"True." Jake lifted Allison to her feet, ready to tie the yellow belt around her waist, but her hand shot out to stop him.

"I can do it myself, thank you very much." She proceeded to wrap it expertly and tie it in a square knot, then looked up at him to receive the proper appreciation.

Jake roared with laughter, and didn't stop as he embraced Allison, swinging her around and around the tatami mat.

"Any karate master would agree that you're ready for advancement," he said, his handsome face glowing with enjoyment.

"Think so?" Allison asked, stepping away from Jake to strut her stuff. "I do look pretty good in yellow, don't you think?"

Jake looked at her, pride and love shining in his eyes.

Sobering, Allison bowed to her *sensei.*

Jake solemnly returned her bow.

"You would look wonderful in anything, Allison McKay," Jake whispered, turning her toward the mirrored wall to see herself.

He placed two hands on Allison's hips and gently pushed the yellow belt lower. His eyes searched her face.

"Marry me?"

"First, there's something I need to know."

"Whatever makes you happy, my love," Jake swore, still watching her warily.

"Do you mind very much if I decide to become a couch potato again? All this excitement is getting to me."

Jake burst into relieved laughter.

"I don't mind. Just so long as I'm the only guy who gets to sit next to you. Now and forever."

Allison sighed, lifting her face for a kiss. "Okay. Now and forever. I know I'll never be the hard-bodied woman you deserve, but promise me something." She cupped his face in her hands. "Could we stop by Taco Hacienda on the way home for a burrito grande?"

"My pleasure," Jake whispered, capturing her lips in a long, satisfying kiss. "Make that two."

ABOUT THE AUTHOR

Adelaide Ferguson is a novelist, essayist, and free-lance writer who lives and works in the Greater Houston area. Ms. Ferguson's business background is in marketing and marketing research, which she left after twenty-five years to write full-time.

Ms. Ferguson is the recipient of numerous awards for poetry and short stories as well. An honors graduate in Psychology from the University of Houston, Ms. Ferguson is widely traveled in the United States, Europe, and Polynesia; she brings both color and cultural insight to her writing.